Fear

Jose Francisco Trevino Chavez

Independently Published

FEAR

Copyright © Jose Francisco Trevino Chavez

All rights reserved.

This is a work of fiction.

Any names, characters, places, and events are products of the author's imagination and are used fictitiously. Any resemblance to persons living or dead is coincidental. Any opinions expressed are those of the characters and should not be confused with the author's. No part of this book may be reproduced in any form or by and means, electronic or mechanical. This includes storage and retrieval systems without written permission from the author, with the exception of brief quotations in reviews.

Published 2024
ISBN: 978-1-960534-12-5 (Paperback)
ASIN: (eBook)

Contents

MONSTER	VII
THE BANQUET	1
HUNGER	29
THE JOURNEY	47
DINNER FOR TWO	68
DEAD TONGUES	77
PATIENT #41	123
TIMMY IS BACK	143
A FATHER'S PAIN	179
SPECIAL THANKS	223

To my mother, she taught me how to face my fears. Thank you, I love you.

MONSTER

by Jose Francisco Trevino Chavez

Does yours have teeth? Claws? Perhaps tentacles?
It really doesn't matter.
It changes from person to person and culture to culture; the nature of the beast.
It's unbound by logic and feeds off our imagination.
It lurks in the shadows and toys with us, letting us see it but only in small glimpses from the corner of our eyes. Sometimes, it has no body whatsoever. Sometimes, it's merely an idea.
But it has haunted mankind since the very beginning.
The only advice I can give you is this:
Your monster cannot harm you unless you allow it.
It lives under your skin, but will never touch you.
It makes your heart skip, but will never make it stop.
Its name is fear.

THE BANQUET

by Jose Francisco Trevino Chavez

At one thirty in the afternoon, the sound of the doorbell woke up Nathan, a twenty-two-year-old sloth of a man. The noise brought his eyes open, his vision blurry and head pounding. He pushed himself off his bed thinking, *"Who the fuck is it?"*

His room still held the smell of cheap liquor and stale pizza. As he fumbled across the hallway of his neglected apartment, he caught a glimpse of the mailman leaving a package. Nathan opened the front door and slowly reached for it. Somehow, he didn't fall to the floor despite the hellish hangover tormenting him.

He took the package to his kitchen and with a sloppy swipe of his only sharp kitchen knife, it opened. He didn't remember ordering anything online. He glanced at the note and saw it had no name or address but his own. The package contained a large wooden box; it was polished and the grain looked to be of a high-quality wood.

"Damn, fancy-ass box." Nathan said to himself as he continued inspecting it. Inside was an envelope, Nathan opened it and saw an alabaster-colored invitation for a dinner party. It read:

Dear Nathan Andrews,

You are invited to attend a once-in-a-lifetime opportunity. This invitation is for a special banquet where most of the attendees are quite wealthy. The reason you are invited is so that you can change your life, to mold it into what you have always dreamed it could be. Our usual attendees enjoy assisting people such as yourself in starting a business or with other projects such as recording a studio album or staging an art exhibition.

The choice is yours. Should you choose to attend, just take the cellphone inside and turn it on. The rest is as simple as following directions.

Sincerely,
your new friend,
The Host

Nathan's brow dipped as he finished reading the beautiful invitation. Normally, he would have been insulted as The Host had essentially called him *poor*, however, the invitation looked to be handwritten in calligraphy so it felt more like a backhanded compliment.

He scoffed at the idea and thought, "Oh yeah, like this is *actually* real." With so many online scams nowadays, Nathan hardly believed in anything or anyone but himself. He took a deeper look into the package and under the fancy tissue paper he found a flip phone akin to the style from the early two thousands out of its package but with the plastic film still attached to the outer screen.

The sight of it sent him to his middle school days and how he loved his little flip phone. A smile sneaked its way onto his face. Out of nostalgia he flipped it open and held down the power button. The screen exploded to life as it turned bright white and the company logo danced across.

A few seconds later the cell phone started to ring. Nathan closed the phone and ignored the call. He dug deeper in the package but there was nothing left. The phone stopped ringing, Nathan's eyes shifted back to the phone and he took a look at the call history. He noticed that the number was local. He called back and waited.

The line rang three times only to hang up a second later. Nathan laughed and said, "Shit Nathan, you must still be drunk. This is clearly a scam." He leaned back on the kitchen chair and sighed from relief.

He stood up a second later and went to the fridge. He swung the door open only to see a vast wasteland of empty takeout containers and beer cans. The smell seemed to have come from about three months back.

His hand reached out toward the far back of the fridge and by some miracle he found the last unopened beer can. His fingernail latched on to the can's tab and pulled back. *FIZZ! CRACK!* The smell of beer filled Nathan's nostrils. They flared instinctively; his mouth watered. He brought the blue can with white lettering up to his puckering lips.

The cold bitterness followed by a slight sourness of the beer brought a wide smile to Nathan's face. As the pounding in his head started dissipating once he downed the first half of his beer, he exhaled and thought, "Now for a proper breakfast. Where to, Nathan?" With nothing coming to mind he sat back down. He knew he had little money left and didn't want to waste it.

His stomach rumbled, protesting Nathan's life choices. Nathan knew this wouldn't be a problem if he hadn't quit his job at the pharmacy, but he just couldn't deal with people's attitudes anymore. Especially boomers who still couldn't figure out how to use the damn credit card reader.

RING! RING! RING! The phone demanded Nathan's attention with every ring. His head turned to it and this time he answered in time.

"Hello?"

"Hello, Nathan Andrews I presume?" A calm deep voice asked through the phone. "Hello? Are you there, Nathan?"

"Uh, yes. Yes, I'm here. Who is this?" Nathan replied nervously.

The man on the other side of the phone chuckled and said, "It's alright Nathan, there's nothing to be afraid of. I'm the host of the special banquet. Since you answered my call, can I safely assume that you will be attending?"

"I-I don't know. Look, I've never heard of this banquet thing and it sounds like a scam." Nathan replied as honestly as he had been in a while. He wasn't this honest when he broke up with his last girlfriend for getting fat. He just told her it wasn't working out.

"That's no problem, Nathan. I'll be honest with you since you are being honest with me. Of course you haven't heard of us. We like to keep it that way. If we were to advertise, then we would have an overwhelming number of people calling."

"Yeah, okay, I see your point. But how do I know I can trust you?"

The man replied. "Trust doesn't come easy son, but I'll tell you something. Society runs on trust. Think of how many times you or I have gone to a store and paid with a large bank note. The cashier hands us our change and we rarely count it. Or how about the stranger we speak to on the elevator? They could be a serial killer for all we know. Would it help if I gave you my name?"

"Yes," Nathan instantly blurted out.

"My name is Martin Tyler. I wrote the invitation on the package. I am "*The Host.*" Feel better now? Look me up online, I'll wait," Mr Tyler said.

Nathan stood up and walked to his room, his eyes scanning for his smartphone. The bed, practically deconstructed and still holding onto most of Nathan's dead skin cells from when he bought it years ago. *Not there*, he thought. His abandoned bean bag chair, which at this point was mostly buried in dirty clothes, had last night's jeans.

Nathan took them with a clean sweeping motion and reached into the pockets. *There you are*, he thought as his fingers grabbed onto the smartphone. He pulled it out of its denim prison and typed in the given name. To his surprise, Martin Tyler turned out to be the C.F.O. of a well-known software company.

"Describe yourself." Nathan then said to Martin.

"Slender, forty-seven, tall, slick blonde hair. Satisfied yet?" Martin replied.

Nathan's jaw swung open. *He's not lying. It's really him*, Nathan thought. His smartphone buzzed in his hand. A notification popped up informing him of a deposit in his bank account. It was seven hundred dollars.

"Did you just send me money?" Nathan asked.

Mr Tyler laughed. "Yes, Nathan, yes I did. Think of it as a way to entice you to join us. What do you say?" Mr. Tyler's hearty laugh carried an odd warmth to it that made Nathan simultaneously lower and raise his guard.

He took a moment before replying, "I really appreciate the gesture, Mr. Tyler. And to answer your question, yes, I will be attending."

"That's wonderful, son. I'll see you soon then. Oh, one last thing. Formal wear is required. Goodbye Nathan."

The call ended before Nathan could reply. His mind now wondered, *where do I get a suit from?*

His flip phone chimed and his eyes read the new text. It was the address for a men's clothing store and an appointment time.

Just as Nathan was leaving the men's clothing store with his new suit, his new flip phone started to vibrate.

"Hello?" Nathan said, but instead of Mr Tyler's hearty voice, a sweet and high-pitched female voice replied.

"Nathan Andrews, please follow these instructions exactly as I tell you if you wish to attend the banquet. Walk over to the nearest bus stop and wait for a black SUV. When it finds you, it will park directly across from you. You'll have to get in it, and once you do, just follow the driver's instructions. Thank you."

And just like that, the call ended. Nathan did as he was told and found the nearest bus stop. He waited for about twenty minutes before the SUV appeared. He stared at it for a second before getting in. The vehicle was so clean, it was almost like staring into a mirror on wheels. Nathan sat in the right rear seat.

The driver sat still, his pitch-black hair and shades contrasting with his nearly paper-white skin. He wore a gray suit. His right arm swung back and handed Nathan a note. It read:

Under your seat is a metal box. Place both phones inside it and place the black cloth over your head. Neither parts are negotiable. No harm will come to you.

Despite a creeping fear lurching its ugly head, Nathan did as he was told. Nathan pushed the fear away thinking, *Chill Nathan, you know who's involved. Besides, who would want you? You look like shit.* The driver took off as soon as the black cloth bag was over his head. Wearing the bag, telling time was near impossible. Nausea set in, his stomach contracting and expanding over and over, his mouth overflowing with saliva.

The vehicle stopped just as Nathan started heaving. The bag was ripped off his head, and the driver handed Nathan another note to read. He swallowed the mess in his mouth and took the note. Now that he could see his surroundings, nausea retreated a few seconds later. He read the note and followed its instructions.

He took his phones out of the metal box and exited the vehicle. Across from him was a wide white mansion with gothic architecture. The design clashed with the color, creating a feeling of forced cleanliness. Nathan counted three floors, assuming it had no lower levels. From the number of vehicles, it appeared that Nathan was the fourth guest to arrive.

He walked to the front door and an older gentleman allowed him in. The man wore a black suit and was around his late sixties. His gray hair and worn skin carried a pair of calm olive eyes. He led Nathan to a lounge where the other guests mingled. Once there, he read a note on a small table atop a metal box that said:

Place phones inside the metal box. They will be returned to you after the banquet. Thank you.

Just as he finished placing his phones inside, a voice reached his ears.

"Fresh meat!" said a large man as he pointed to Nathan. "I'm joking son, I just meant that you are new here is all. What's your name?"

Nathan stared at him, laughing off the comment. "Nathan Andrews, sir. A pleasure."

The man shook Nathan's hand. "No son, the pleasure is mine. Tell me Nathan, why did you decide to attend? What do you hope to gain tonight?"

The man held eye contact with Nathan as he waited for an answer. Nathan cleared his throat.

"Honestly, I don't know. I'm pretty good in the kitchen. Perhaps I could start a little cafe. Something simple but inviting."

The man nodded and smiled politely. He pointed at Nathan. "I like that. In my opinion, everyone should know how to cook at least a little. I also like your attitude, most people want to become celebrities. You know, actors, musicians, and such. Not you, you seem to want stability. I'll be seeing you later Nathan. I suggest you get to know the other *benefactors* here."

Nathan nodded and smiled as the man walked away. He took a look across the vast room and tried to recognize anyone. Most of the people there weren't people he knew nor recognized from tv or anywhere else for that matter.

Then, Nathan spotted *her*.

He was certain it had to be her, from her tall and thin figure to the way she carried herself across the room. Her pale blue eyes were held above dark half circles, the contrast made it look like her eyes weren't blue but light gray.

Nathan started walking toward her. He never expected his favorite singer to be there. Despite having the type of appearance that hints at junky, Nathan had no dangerous vices. His only weakness was music. His drinking was only for the weekends, even if it was a bit more than one person should drink. As he got closer to her, he tried to think of what to say.

Just before he could grab her attention, a chiming bell kidnapped everyone's attention.

As everyone turned their heads toward the noise, a man stood out atop the stairs at the end of the room. The man was a slender, blonde man. Nathan recognized him as soon as his eyes landed on him. It was the host, Martin Tyler.

The room exploded with applause. Nathan turned around and noticed that about three-quarters of the people in the room were clapping. The few that weren't, carried confusion on their faces. It was safe for Nathan to assume that they were the "*special guests*" Martin mentioned earlier.

"Thank you, you are too kind. For the newcomers, I am the host of this banquet. My name is Martin Tyler. Please follow me to the banquet hall. Let us begin this wonderful evening," Martin said, introducing himself. Everyone followed Martin up the wide and elegant stairway.

At the top of the second floor was a vast rectangular table with an enormous variety of food. The large room was dimly lit by candlelight, the room's white base color and golden details screaming luxury. Several servants led the guests to their seats, most of their choosing, others guided to certain benefactors.

Nathan was unfortunately seated at opposite ends of the table from *Eloise Fernand*. Once everyone was seated, Martin, at the head of the table, stood up and began speaking.

"I will now explain how this will work. Most of you have been seated with your potential goal in mind. Of course, if we have calculated incorrectly, you are more than welcome to change seats. The only rules here are the following. The first: everyone must have a wonderful meal. The second: everyone's lives must have changed significantly after this evening. That being said, *bon appétit.*"

"Nathan, I'm glad to have a seat close to yours. Allow me to properly introduce myself, my name is *Kenneth Morrison*."

Nathan heard the hearty voice coming from across the table, his eyes shifting over to the voice's owner, the large man from earlier. He smiled at Nathan as he sat down and rested his cane against the table. His tan suit was complimented well by his class ring that held a deep red garnet.

The two smiled. Servers approached the guests, and a server asked for his order. Nathan took a look around and saw lamb chops with mint jelly, beef Wellington, a pork loin roasted in clay, a large tray with Cornish game hens, and other assorted dishes he couldn't see clearly from his seat.

Kenneth cleared his throat and chimed in, "Forgive my intrusion Nathan, but I highly recommend the clay-roasted pork loin. Believe me when I say that you have never tasted something quite like it. Everyone will inevitably try it, so why not start there?"

Kenneth pointed directly at it with an eager smile. Nathan took a look at it and nodded to the server. A few seconds later the server started preparing Nathan a plate. While the server did that, Nathan started chatting with Mr. Morrison.

"So Mr. Morrison, what do you do for a living?"

Kenneth placed his water down. "I work for the government, as a kind of policing."

"You're with the police? Really? You kind of look more like a politician." Nathan's face showed genuine interest.

Kenneth shook his head. "Not quite police. It's similar, only higher risk."

"Oh okay, so FBI then?" Nathan pressed on. Kenneth shook his head as he took another sip of water, Nathan's server arrived with his plate and set it down for him. The smell took his attention, his mouth watered and his eyes were forced down.

His plate presented him with two beautiful slices of pork loin on a bed of roasted potatoes and carrots.

To Nathan's surprise, the pork was a bit darker than he expected. Kenneth stared at Nathan with intense anticipation. His eyes widened, his hands tightened around his silverware, and his mouth arched, creating a tense smile. Nathan smiled back at Kenneth and started to slice the meat into a decent bite. His fork pierced the juicy pork, followed by a piece of potato and carrot. He brought the bite to his mouth and started chewing.

The taste was exquisite, salts and herbs singing in his mouth. The potato's texture was perfect, with a slight crunch before a soft center announced itself. The natural sweetness of the carrot contrasted the meat, a delicate and pleasant balance.

The flavor, however, was unexpected. It was more akin to that of a full-bodied veal than pork.

"What did I tell you? Incredible isn't it?" Kenneth asked just after Nathan finished his bite. "Now please take a sip of your Pinot Noir. That's true bliss son!" Nathan grabbed his wine and took the recommended sip.

The miniature wave of wine crashed in Nathan's mouth, leaving hints of vanilla, cherry, and an unidentified earthiness Nathan knew he had tasted before, but just couldn't place his finger on it.

He nodded at Kenneth. "You're right. This is delicious. I've never tasted pork like this. I wonder what the chef used."

"He'll never reveal his secrets unless you become a *member*. Otherwise, you'll never know. Most of the people invited here don't have what it takes to become one." Kenneth replied, his face becoming firm and harsh as the words escaped his mouth.

Nathan asked as he prepared his second bite. "And how exactly does a guest become a member? I barely have enough money for myself."

Kenneth replied with his mouth still chewing his pork loin. "I'm not so sure. He would be the only one able to answer that question.."

His finger pointed directly at the opposite end of the table. Nathan turned to follow the finger and saw who Kenneth was referring to. It was the host, Martin, who crossed gazes with Nathan. Martin politely raised his glass of red wine toward Nathan and mouthed "cheers" before returning to his conversation with Eloise.

Something about Martin's gaze didn't feel right to Nathan.

Kenneth took Nathan's hand. "You should go talk to him," he said. "You've already passed the first step."

"What are you talking about? I haven't done anything." Nathan replied, slowly pulling back his hand, but Kenneth wasn't letting go. Instead, his grip tightened.

He smiled at Nathan. "Come on, I'll introduce you."

Nathan was practically dragged out of his seat as Kenneth took him to the other end of the table. As Nathan stumbled across the room, he noticed something odd. Most of the guests were either offered or served pork loin. Nathan counted at least four entire pork loins from which they served from.

"Martin, this boy wants to know how to be a member." Kenneth said loudly as he and Nathan approached Martin. Eloise stopped talking and gave Kenneth a deadly glare.

Martin smiled. "Does he? How interesting. Tell me, Nathan, how are you finding this banquet? Do you like it?"

Nathan nodded. He was nervous. Something about Martin's energy felt cold, predatory.

Martin smiled kindly. "I'm glad. Allow me to introduce you to a very close friend of mine. This is—"

"Eloise Fernand. She's spectacular," Nathan interrupted. "I'm a big fan, it's an honor to meet you, Miss Fernand. My name's Nathan Andrews."

His voice quivered lightly. Eloise smiled and shook his hand. Martin stood up and reached for another seat, then offered Nathan his, which Nathan immediately took. Sitting next to Eloise made Nathan forget about the creeping feeling on the back of his neck. The man was mesmerized by her.

She leaned in close to whisper. "Do you know what it means to be a member, Nathan?"

He smiled like an idiot and shook his head.

Eloise turned to Martin. "Are we even accepting new members?"

He stared at her, his face calm and analytical. "Sure we are."

Kenneth whispered something to Martin. He smiled widely and turned to Nathan.

"Kenneth tells me you liked the pork loin. What exactly did you like about it?"

The question reminded Nathan of what he saw on his way there from his initial seat. He discreetly turned to the other guests and saw nearly everyone else eating the pork loin.

He returned his gaze to Martin. "Everything is different about it. The taste isn't what I expected. It was more like veal, not pork."

Martin nodded, his smile widening. "Yes, you're right. The pigs used are special, they are raised in very particular conditions. Did you know that pigs are rather smart? They're like humans."

A few chairs to the left, a female guest gasped. Martin, Eloise, and Kenneth paid no attention to her, but Nathan couldn't help but turn.

The gasp morphed into a scream. She pushed herself back, her chair sliding across the granite floor. Martin stood up and made his way to the frightened guest. She was a slim Asian woman, twenty-four or so. Her hair was short and deep black, the kind of black that turned blue under lighting.

Martin gently placed his hand on her shoulder. "What's the matter?" He asked.

The poor woman couldn't stop shaking. "The pork, it, it has a name tattooed. It's not right it—"

"Calm down, sweetie, let's talk to the chef. I'm certain there is a perfectly reasonable explanation for this." Martin told her as he guided her out of the dining room and into the kitchen. As they walked, he snapped his fingers and a server immediately removed her plate from sight.

Nathan stepped forward, but didn't make it three steps before Eloise's hand firmly grasped his arm and pulled him back. He fell back into his seat and stared at her with surprise. For such a thin woman, she was quite strong. Her piercing blue eyes saw right through him.

"Don't be scared, Nathan. I won't bite, I only bite when needed."

Martin led the frightened guest to the kitchen on the top floor. Once there, he said to her, "Look, there he is. Let's get him to explain what happened. Would that make you feel better, Sue?"

The guest nodded, then paused. "How do you know my name? We never spoke. When I answered the call for the invitation, I spoke to a woman."

"I made certain that I'd know every guest here. What kind of host would I be if I didn't know everyone invited?" Martin reassured her with a small and discreet smile. Sue nodded, as everything Martin said made sense. He led her directly to where the chef was.

The kitchen was bustling with near-clockwork precision. The chef was a short square of a man, his face carrying cold calculating stares, his hands riddled with scars. As he moved from end to end of the kitchen, he saw Martin. The chef stopped dead in his tracks and smiled at Martin.

"Mr Tyler, how can I assist you? Was there something wrong with the food?"

Martin kept his smile intact. "Bernard, the food tastes heavenly, as always. This is my guest, Sue. She has something she'd like to know. You see, on the pork loin she was served there was a ... *tattoo* was it?"

She nodded, her eyes never making direct contact with either man.

Martin continued. "The sight of it frightened her. I brought her here so you could reassure her that everything is fine."

"I see, my apologies, Miss." Bernard replied. "Give me the opportunity to show you what happened. Follow me." Filled with embarrassment, Bernard kept his eyes low to the ground. He led Sue and Martin to the walk-in freezer, and opened it.

"The pigs are at the back. The floor is color coded, the yellow perimeter being for pork."

Sue froze, her face bouncing from the deep end of the freezer back to Bernard.

Martin placed his right hand on Sue's back. "I'll go with you," he said to reassure her. Sue was completely underdressed for the freezer, her black dress having no back. *CLACK, CLACK!* Her heels complained as they struck the metal floor.

Sue and Martin followed the yellow line. Once there, they saw several pig carcasses hanging on large metal hooks. A few of them had a strange symbol stamped on their skin with blue ink, the color matching the one Sue was served.

"The pigs used for tonight's dinner have the needed stamp of approval," Bernard explained. "The ink is bright blue, which simply means it passed the inspection. Was that what you were hoping to hear, Miss?"

"Oh, um... I guess so," Sue replied. "I just thought I saw something else. Something like a name with a flower." She was so certain of what she had seen, and now she saw the situation for what it was.

Martin extended his hand out to her. "Come, the other guests should know about this misunderstanding."

Sue smiled and stepped forward as she reached for his hand. The lighting inside the freezer was mostly bright, the only exception being the dense shadows the hanging meat cast across the floor. These shadows hid a patch of ice that Sue's right foot stepped directly onto.

As her weight shifted, the floor slid from under her. Sue fell back, her hands reaching aimlessly. Her body slammed backward into half of a hanging pork. The chains jingled, and the carcass swung from side to side. A wet thud came from behind, and Sue turned only to see a thawing human arm.

The light caught it. It had pale skin, and about a foot away was the headless torso it belonged to. There was a second of tangible silence, before a blood-curdling scream erupted from Sue. She frantically stood up and tried to escape the freezer.

Martin swung his right arm, catching the nearest meat hook, and swung it directly into Sue's head. Her body snapped back, and an odd numbness spread across the back of her head. She felt a liquid warmth dribble down her back. Once the numbness faded, a strong wave of pain burst out.

Her legs gave out, and her body fell but only a few inches. Martin walked up to her.

"Oh Sue, why did you have to slip? Now look at yourself. You're hanging from a hook like these pigs." Martin kneeled down and swiped his finger across the puddle of blood under Sue. He brought his finger to his nose and took the aroma in.

"Mr Tyler, is everything alright?" Nathan asked when Martin returned to his seat. "Where is the girl you left with?"

Martin nodded politely. He picked up his wineglass and a knife, stood up, and struck them together.

"Everyone, if I could please have your attention. Everything has been cleared up. What the young lady named Sue saw was nothing but a stamp of approval. Unfortunately, the fright wore her out and she decided to return home. That is all, you may return to your meal."

Everyone continued as if nothing happened. Nathan saw Martin and Eloise exchange a peculiar look. *Is he lying?*

Eloise caught him staring. "What's wrong Nathan?" She asked. "Why the funny look?"

Nathan went pale and shook his head. "No, look. It's just...why would she leave?"

Eloise nodded and turned to Martin. "Nathan is right, it really doesn't make sense to just leave," she said with a smile. "Why don't you tell him how it happened?" Martin stared stiffly at Eloise, his smile was nowhere to be found.

"Didn't he want to become a member?" she said. "Test him."

"You're right Eloise. Come, Nathan, there's only one last test for you," Martin said, his face dark, serious. "I hardly doubt that the other guests have what it takes." Nathan followed. As they left, Nathan saw Eloise stand and call the attention of the other guests.

"I hope you guys are ready for the final course. I—"

The rest of what Eloise said was cut off from Nathan's earshot, as the kitchen was too noisy to hear her. Bernard sampled a dish, saying "she" was lovely.

He caught Martin entering his kitchen with his peripheral vision and turned to face him. "Mr. Tyler, how can I help you this time?"

As he walked toward him, Martin gently waved. "I'm here to introduce you to Nathan. He wants to become a member."

Bernard's eyes shot open.

"I know, I know," Martin said. "However, Eloise suggested that he be tested."

"Well... Eloise is keen on such people. If you insist," said Bernard. He turned to Nathan. "A pleasure meeting you. You should know that to become a member, one must cross a certain line. Once you know what must be done, there's no going back. After becoming a member though, it's smooth sailing from there. Nathan hated how that sounded, yet Bernard seemed like a good man. His voice was calm, his eyes never showed any animosity or danger. Everything he did was completely normal. But then why did every fiber of Nathan's being scream danger to him?

Nathan pushed the feeling aside. He thought about how he hated his life. No job, money, stability, or love. He couldn't see where his life could go worse if he tried. If there was a time to turn things around, it would be now.

Nathan looked up. "Yes, I want to continue."

Bernard and Martin shared a smile and took Nathan to a small table. They sat him down, placed a small plate with what looked like five chicken wings. The wings were glazed in a brown sauce. The smell was sweet with a hint of citrus.

Wings? Odd for a fancy dinner, but alright.

Both men stared at Nathan.

"There's no turning back," Martin said. "You must eat at least two of these *wings*."

"Is this a trick?" Nathan asked. "Like, are they crazy spicy?"

"Bernard would never do such a thing to food, especially his own. Allow me to demonstrate," Martin replied as he ate one of the wings. There was no odd expression on his face nor any redness. He smiled. "Satisfied?"

Nathan nodded and took one of the wings. The sauce was thin and sticky. It had an oil base. The meat was nowhere to be found. It was more like eating skin. The taste was wonderful, clean protein with a delicate sauce.

A few seconds later, it was gone. Nathan moved on to the next wing. This one had much more meat. As he ate, he could see Martin and Bernard exchanging stares. Bernard whispered something to Martin, who nodded in response.

Since the wings were so good, Nathan continued. He placed the clean bone on his plate and kept eating. At around the halfway point of the third wing, Nathan noticed that the second bone was odd. Its shape was curved and the tips were nearing a perfect cylinder. Nathan placed his half-eaten wing down and took the aforementioned bone.

He took a close look at it. He saw blade marks on it. Bone saw, to be exact. That's when he realized it wasn't a wing, but a partial rib. He compared the rib bone to the first bone. Nathan could see they weren't the same.

That's strange, looks like a hand bone. No, it can't be. That's illegal, it's wrong.

"So?" Martin asked. "Figured it out?"

Nathan looked up to Martin's pleasant smile but it was gone, a dark grin in its place. "Figured out what?" Nathan's voice was high and cracking.

Martin grasped Nathan's arm. His grip was strong, to the point where it hurt. Martin replied with a serious tone. "What the dish is? Kenneth mentioned you had a delicate palate. He also told me you nearly pinpointed the pork loin. So humor me. What did you just eat?"

Nathan tried pulling his arm back but it was no use, Martin wouldn't let go. Martin shook his head, waiting for an answer. Nathan thought it through, and his mouth opened but had no voice.

Martin leaned in close to Nathan, "Come on, I'm sure you know. I think you're just scared because you *loved* the taste."

Nathan started shedding tears, his head dipped. His body trembled and he murmured something Martin couldn't make out.

Martin turned to Bernard, "Did you catch that?"

"No sir, I didn't." Something about the way Bernard replied, as if the situation was normal, made Nathan fear much more than the possibility of having eaten something *morally* wrong. He feared for his life.

Martin turned back to Nathan. "Answer the question."

Nathan inhaled sharply and said, "I... I think I ate human flesh." Nathan held his eyes shut tightly.

Martin clapped. "Exactly! Kenneth was right. You do have a sensitive palate. Most people can't figure it out. Now that you know, I have to ask one last thing of you. The last step is to choose your next meal."

Nathan locked eyes with Martin. "Are you asking me to choose who to eat?"

Martin nodded with a sinister smile, "Precisely, child. You are to return to the dining hall and point out who you want *us* to eat. After we're done dining, you'll officially be a member."

Martin pulled Nathan up to his feet and led him back to the dining hall. Bernard returned to work after eating one of Nathan's leftover "*wings.*" Dessert was next.

Nathan was seated next to Eloise again. To his left was Kenneth, who wore a twisted grin. Eloise on the other hand barely looked at Nathan. At this point, Nathan didn't really care if she noticed him. His mind played one phrase over and over like a scratched record.

This isn't real, it has to be a nightmare. This isn't real, it has to be a nightmare. THIS ISN'T REAL, IT HAS TO BE A NIGHTMARE!

Martin placed a hand on Nathan's shoulder and whispered. "Calm down, your problems will disappear soon. We take care of our own."

Nathan said nothing, he was too busy trying not to scream.

Eloise had boredom written across her face, her eyes bouncing from guest to guest. The servers went into the kitchen, and returned with dessert. Everyone was served the same thing: a small bowl filled with a rich chocolate pudding accompanied by two ladyfingers and garnished with a fresh slice of blood orange.

Martin stood up. "I truly hope each and every one of you savors this wonderful dessert," he announced. "It was something I stumbled across in my youth traveling through Italy. Anyway, that's enough of me talking. Enjoy."

Eloise leaned toward Nathan. "I'm not much of a dessert person," she whispered. "Martin loves this dessert and he insisted I try it out. I liked it, but didn't think too much of it. Then I found out the secret ingredient. It was originally supposed to be pig blood, but Bernard uses human blood. Try it, you'll love it. In the meantime, I'll be in the ladies' room. Excuse me."

Nathan stared at the pudding as Eloise walked away, the dark pool acting like a small black mirror. The reflection of Nathan's face was contorted to the point of visible pain. Sweat dripped down Nathan's face, the cold liquid crawling down like an interloping spider across his face.

The bead of sweat crashed into the dark pool of thick chocolate pudding. Nathan could barely hear the sound of silverware clattering about, his brain instead focusing on the ever-growing thumps of his heart. *THUMP! THUMP! THUMP!* His heartbeat was deafening. Every thump was not only heard, but felt across his chest, throat, and head.

His eyes drifted to the pudding again. They caught his reflected gaze and for just a brief moment, Nathan's reflection smiled at him. Time slowed, his fear melted away, and was replaced by a sudden surge of power. His body ceased sweating, his vision sharpened, and hearing cleared.

Survive, Nathan. Power comes at a cost. Embrace it.

"So, have you decided yet?" Martin asked. The question brought Nathan back to earth.

He shook his head to Martin, then turned back to the guests and scanned the dining table. The other eight guests were quite different from each other. There was a large round man with olive skin. His face had a long, thin nose and small eyes. *Not a chance in hell I'd pick him.*

A few seats from him was a petite woman. Her flame-red hair was curly and wild, clashing with her shy body language. She constantly stared at the door and any possible exits. *Not enough of a chase,* Nathan rationalized.

At the far end of the table was a stick of a man. His long frame acted like more of a coat rack than a body for his clothes. Nathan shook his head. *No nutritional value.*

He continued scanning the table when he saw the perfect prey. A tall, athletic man, and his light brown skin was perfect. His muscle tone was developed but not overdone. Nathan met eyes with him, and both smiled. Nathan slowly turned toward Martin while maintaining eye contact with his prey. "What's his name, Mr. Tyler? I *want* him." Nathan asked.

Martin raised his eyebrows. "His name's Hector Suarez, are you sure you want him? He was an athlete, but an injury stopped his career."

Nathan stared at the man. "That's my pick."

Martin nodded with a smile, and Kenneth discreetly handed Nathan a knife from underneath the table. Nathan stared at it.

"Do it. Hunt your prey," Kenneth said. "As soon as you act, so will the servers."

Nathan slowly stood up and walked towards Hector. *One quick slice across the throat and it'll be over. From here on out no more problems.*

Nathan felt his heart pounding and his hands sweating, but his mind was set. His goal was right there, all he needed to do was take it. Every step felt eternal, the guests continued eating their dessert, none the wiser.

A few steps away from Hector, Nathan looked around and saw an empty seat. He then remembered who it belonged to. *She freaked out, Martin took her to the kitchen and never came back. Did she figure it out? How can I trust them? I don't know them. I don't know them!* Nathan thought.

Before Nathan knew it, he was standing right behind Hector. The person sitting across from Hector stared at Nathan, Hector noticed and turned around.

"Can I help you?" Hector asked.

Nathan slowly leaned close to Hector. "It's a trap. They want me to kill you."

Nathan gently poked Hector with the tip of his knife. Hector saw it and his body tightened.

Nathan noticed that the man beside them saw Nathan's intentions. He plunged the knife into the man's neck and screamed out, "Everyone run! These people are monsters!"

Everyone stopped eating and stared at Nathan. Confusion filled the air. A few guests noticed the injured man and started running, while a few others froze in their seats. Nathan ran for the stairs and managed to get away from two servers trying to catch him. Hector was too fast for the servers to stop him, and as he ran, Nathan took a few looks back.

The guests that froze were caught by the nearest servers and quickly killed with the nearest knife. Martin caught Nathan's gaze, shaking his head like a disappointed father. Hector flew past Nathan.

BANG! BANG!

FEAR

Hector fell to the floor motionless. Nathan fell too; his leg felt numb and hot. He looked down and saw his thigh bleeding. The sound of high heels got closer from behind Nathan.

"You shouldn't have done that. You could have been one of us. Oh well, I don't really care," He turned around and as soon as he faced Eloise, her heel slammed against his face. Eloise slid the slit of her dress to the side and holstered her pistol back to her thigh. Everything went black after that.

Nathan's head pounded away, his mouth was gagged, his eyes bound.

"Oh good, you're awake. Let me take this off." Martin's voice was filled with glee. The bright kitchen lights blinded Nathan as his eye covers were removed. He, Eloise, Bernard, and Kenneth stood across from Nathan.

"You are the first guest to cause this much trouble. Sue, the guest that nearly caused a scene, didn't give me this much trouble. But you," Martin said. "I've done this for decades. You know, my family started these banquets. I'll get to the point. Nathan, you ruined my dinner. Now you'll be my dinner. Please look down."

Nathan looked, his vision having mostly adjusted to the lighting by then. He immediately started hyperventilating, then shrieked through the ball gag. Nathan saw why he couldn't feel his limbs. He was nothing more than a torso now. He thrashed about, but it was useless.

Eloise smiled at him, clearly enjoying his struggle and panic. She turned to Martin and asked, "I know you want to kill him, but may I take the first bite?"

"By all means, ladies first," Martin replied. Eloise took a fork and knife, walked up to Nathan, and started carving out a piece of his abdomen. Nathan's muffled screams barely escaped the ball gag.

She took a bite, then licked her lips. "Let's dig in." As soon as she said it, everyone joined in.

HUNGER

by Jose Francisco Trevino Chavez

The green lasers outline a group of people dancing under the strobing orange and blue lights of the nightclub. I evaluate each of them carefully. After all, hidden somewhere amongst them lies my next meal. I take a deep breath. The usual mixture of sweat, hormones, narcotics, and countless perfumes fill my nostrils. I take another breath, this time I try to separate the junk from the quality food.

My brows rise as I pick up the scent of something special buried in the crowd. My lips twist into a smile as I salivate. I close my eyes and try to hone into this delicacy's exact location. Easier said than done when I have to ignore the powerful punching of the bassline hitting my chest from Mascarpone's "Suicide" playing at a deafening volume. But it's not the first time I hunt at a nightclub.

I follow the intoxicating scent. Each step is placed with rhythmic caution as I weave through the dancing crowd. I've gotten good at traversing unnoticed through crowds. The scent grows as I get closer. I see the source, I run my tongue across my teeth from one fang to the other. Long dark hair, short tight dress with boots. A common attire but I know better than to judge my meals by their wrapper.

I dance my way into her field of view. I get close—intoxicatingly close—my heart rate increases as I finally identify her blood type, O negative. I smile at her when she finally looks my way. She smiles back, and we dance. I exaggerate my lip movement as I mouth to her, "Buy you a drink?"

She does the same replying, "Sure."

We dance our way to the bar, I inhale sharply, analyzing her breath, and tell her, "Let me guess ... vodka cranberry?"

Her eyes widen slightly as she nods. "How'd you know? Been watching me?"

I smile and shake my head. "No, just got here. Lucky guess." I turn to the bartender and order. A few moments later, I'm handed a vodka cranberry and a rum and cola. I hand her her drink and wait for her to sit before I do. I feel the first warning. A slight pressure on my stomach. I expected this, I haven't eaten in two days. It's hungry.

The song ends, and a second of silence grants us a pleasant respite. I extend my hand to her. "A pleasure, I'm Jude."

"Kat. I'm surprised, I don't get many proper introductions anymore. Such a gentleman," she replies jokingly. "I love this song!" she continues as "Le Glas" by Quinze starts playing.

"Me too," I reply.

Kat stands up and pulls me out of my seat. She starts dancing around me, her body in sync with the beat. Her hair tickles my nose as her back pushes against me. I dance with her, I make sure we aren't too far from our drinks. The last thing I need is an idiot spiking our drinks to get to her. I'm hungry for this one and I won't share.

I grab her waist, her weight falls back even more. Her hands reach behind me and start to wander. First my sides, then hips ultimately settling on my bottom. I smile and brush my lips on her right ear. From this distance, I can practically taste her. I pull my head back and turn her around. Easy Jude, can't eat here. You don't want to cause a scene.

"What's wrong, too fast?" she asks pouting.

I shake my head and smile. I lean in close and say to her ear, "Not here. Too exposed."

She downs her drink and walks me to the men's room. I feel my heart racing. My skin tingles. I feel the skin on my face stretching tightly as I inevitably smile from ear to ear. My meal is serving itself. My overflowing excitement disappears as we enter the restroom and the blue lights hit my eyes. Damn anti-junkie lighting. Can't feed here. I stop without knowing, Kat turns to me saying, "Come on."

I pretend everything is fine and take the lead. I take her into a vacant stall closing the door behind us. I bombard her neck, my lips cover her delicate and sweet skin. I can feel her breathing heavily on me. Somewhere between the music's blasting beats, I hear a quiet moan escape her full lips. I meet her eyes, everything slows down. What's happening? Am I really this hungry? Why am I so excited?

Kat's lips on mine bring me out of my head. I feel her hands roaming across my back. I grab her jaw firmly with one hand while I explore her inner thighs. Her eyes widen as she smiles, she welcomes my hand in. I feel something in me tighten. I grunt, not sure why. Could this be excitement or hunger? I think. Either way she hears it and answers it by pulling my hand further up.

I hear her making a kind of rhythm, moan, pant, pant, moan. Her hands travel straight to the front of my pants, my belt and zipper surrender without hesitation. I spin her around pulling her dress up. Her bottom sticks out, my body follows. We were strangers moments ago, now we're familiar with every inch of each other's body.

The smell of her sweat along with the salt on her skin brushing against my tongue sets me off. I press my mouth on her neck as I feel my fangs unsheath. I slowly press the tip of my fangs on her skin. I hear her giggle, so I continue. I break skin and actually taste her even if it's just a few drops. She's exquisite. The purity of the iron, optimal potassium levels, stable glucose and no drugs to alter her flavor.

My lungs fill to the brim. Despite this nightmarish blue light, my vision sharpens. The familiar euphoria of the feeding starts kicking in then fades due to such a low dose. She takes great care of herself. I feel her hand on my jaw, I ease off her neck and ask her, "Did I hurt you?"

"A little," she responds.

Wrapping my arms around her in a caring hug, I reply, "I didn't mean to. Want me to stop?"

Kat shakes her head saying, "No, I liked it."

"You just get better by the second," I reply as I run my hands across her torso. Are those...? She has abs! That's so hot! Somehow this woman has all my attention, I allow myself to revert back to a mere man once again and enjoy her.

Pleasure rules over us, we mix by pure instinct. Her body twitches, I know she's almost there. I still have a little more to go. Being what I am has its advantages outside of hunting. A loud moan explodes out of her leaving her loose in my arms catching her breath.

I exit her and turn her to me, I finish as we kiss. A warm smile from my part turns into a contagious laugh. The stall vibrates with our giddy ecstasy. I brush her long dark hair back and ask, "Everything alright?"

Kat nods and smiles as she lowers her eyes. I kiss her again and I get my second warning. The pressure on my stomach deepens this time bringing a steady burning sensation. I grab my stomach and wince.

"Are you okay?" she asks.

Nodding, I say, "It's nothing. I'm hungry."

"Let's get out of here. The food here sucks," Kat replies, she takes my hand and walks me out of the stall. The restroom door opens, a large man hurries to a urinal and we slip out before it closes. Once outside and able to hear each other, she asks, "Are you from here, Jude?"

"No, this is my first time in Santa Monica. You?"

"Born and raised. Do you eat meat?" Kat replies. I nod. "Great, there's a great hotdog place by the beach." She takes my arm and walks me to it while resting her head on my shoulder.

Why am I nervous? She's just another meal. Nothing more. I tell myself. I try to clear my head by looking up. The deep blue sky holds up for all to see its twinkling diamonds.

We arrive at the hotdog stand and she says, "I'll order for you."

"Sure. Oh wait, nothing with garlic please," I reply.

She turns back and stares for a full second. "You aren't a vampire, are you?" she asks with a smile.

I smile back, shaking my head. "Guilty as charged. Nah, allergic."

"Oh good, you had me worried for a second." Kat flounces up to the stand and returns with two hotdogs. I dig in, it's gone in three large bites. The taste is good, but food no longer satisfies. It doesn't even slow down the monster hiding right beneath my skin. I wipe my mouth clean with my napkin. My eyes are glued to her. Half of her dog is gone.

She says, still looking at her food, "What? You're staring."

"Am I?"

"Uh, yeah."

"Sorry, I guess I can't stop," I finally confess.

Her laugh launches bits of food my way. A bit of bread bounces off my leather jacket. "Oh, sorry. But, cheesy lines, really?" Kat says.

"Not cheesy when it's real," I respond.

Kat makes a "so-so" gesture.

As soon as she swallows her bite I take her and plant a powerful kiss on her lips. Her gray eyes shoot wide open. "I'm old school, Kat. I despise these current generations and their obsession with doing everything casually. And yes, I realize I sound ninety. Maybe I am ninety. Maybe I'm older. So no, fuck cheesy. It's how I feel. Your beauty distracts me. Deal with it."

Kat stares back silently. She nods, taking a sip of her soda.

Her silence weighs me down. Congratulations dumbass, you ruined any chance you had with her. Nice going. I want to be with her? Yes, quit pretending you don't! I think.

She shakes her head, "No, you're right. We're terrified of committing, of the long term. I'll make you a deal. From now on we only tell the truth." Her hand sticks out waiting for a shake.

"Agreed." I shake her hand. "First things first. How old are you?"

"Twenty-five. What do you do for a living?"

"I'm a chef, I'm here to meet a client."

"Really? What's the job?"

"Dinner party uptown. What do you do?"

"Fashion design, mostly I work with fabrics."

"Sounds interesting. I like fashion," I say to her. Then ask, "Would you show me around the pier? I know it's late, but I'm more comfortable with fewer people around."

Kat takes my arm and says as we walk, "Sure. So you're an introvert?"

"No, not really. I got your attention, didn't I?"

"Yeah, I guess you did. Pretty easily too," she says, squeezing me lightly. A wave of warmth rushes over my face. I smile and she says, "You're blushing! That's adorable."

"Stop, you aren't helping." I block my face with my soda.

She lets go of my arm and walks ahead of me. Turning back, she asks, "What happened to the guy I met at the club? He was confident and relaxed. You are way too deep in your head. Loosen up, Jude, I'm not going anywhere. I like you. A lot."

Oh, thank you! My shoulders drop, I reach out to her and pull her into my arms. "You're right, I'm nervous. I don't hook up with people, ever. But you, your essence drew me in," I confess. That was the truth. Maybe not the whole truth, but close enough.

Her lips curve as her nose crinkles. We walk in lovely silence for a few minutes. We're locked in a relaxed hug. I'm a teen again, back in high school with my first love.

I stop her at the pier to look through one of the many free-use viewers. I look up to the night sky and point to a star. "See that star, Kat? It's actually the planet Venus."

"Oh, cool. Are you a space nerd?" Kat replies as she takes a look through the viewer.

"No, not really. I want to be. If we can see it then it means dawn is almost here. It's late, shit," I say. "I should really get going."

"Okay, now you're really sounding like a vampire." Kat turns to face me.

"I mean I need to sleep even if it's just a few hours. I'm meeting my client today."

With an exaggerated swipe across her forehead, she says, "What a relief! Where are you staying?"

"Over by the funny-looking statue of the—"

Kat interrupts, "The weird purple squiggly thing?"

I nod.

"That's all the way across town. Stay over at my place."

"You sure? I don't want to bother you."

"Nonsense, let's go." She leads me in the right direction. We walk along the pier, and I get the third warning. I slow down taking deep breaths. The deep burning pressure in my stomach

FEAR

worsens to the point of stealing my breath. I stop altogether. Kat turns to me, her round gray eyes meet mine. "What's wrong?"

I straighten up and reply pushing past the bottomless pit inside me, "I'm not feeling too good. I think the hotdog is fighting back."

Kat grabs my hand and takes me to the nearest restrooms. She says, "Just be careful, sometimes there are oddballs in there around nighttime."

I nod as I enter. I stumble over to the sink and splash water on my face. I look at my reflection and see all the signs of prolonged lack of food. My olive skin is thinning, my brown eyes are bloodshot, and I can start to hear my heartbeat. It begs for it, the only thing I need.

The door swings open, and I catch a whiff. I turn out of desperation not expecting much. A drunk guy walks in. He's had everything he could from whichever bar served him. I sniff again. Coke and Molly too. Ugh! He settles himself on a vacant urinal. I cover my nose trying to keep the hotdog down as the restroom air fills with his stench.

A good minute passes as he finishes. He zips his pants and turns towards the sinks, our eyes meet. I maintain eye contact, so does he. We wash our hands without exchanging a single word. The only sound present is the running water falling from the faucets. He dries his hands and leans on the wall behind me. I smile as I finish, hoping it's enough bait. The air shifts, it fills up with something else. A strong and unmistakable scent.

I slowly approach him, he licks his lips in response. I place one hand on his chest and start unbuttoning his shirt. He helps me with my pants. I dive into his chest. His hands go straight to the point. I breathe slowly and focus trying to keep my hunger under his radar. "Yeah? You like my grip, don't you?" he says, his smile dripping with arrogance.

"Shh," I say, turning him around. I undo his pants and pull his head back by the hair. He presses his body into mine. I run my lips across his neck, one of my hands travels around his chest while the other slips into his pants. I close my eyes and let my hands rely on muscle memory. Up, down, twist, and so on.

His flavors are worlds apart from Kat's. They're stronger and lack layers. Comparing them is like comparing a subpar grilled steak seasoned only with salt versus a citrus glazed salmon infused with rosemary wrapped in tea leaves. I feel his core tense up just as he melts in my hands.

The restroom door cracks open and I hear, "Jude? You okay?" Kat's cute raspy voice catches me off guard.

I grip tightly, too tight. He grunts, and I whisper, "Sorry." I yell out to her, "Yeah, I'm fine. I'll be right out."

"Girlfriend?" he asks.

"No. Not yet," I reply almost by instinct.

"What about me? Does she know?" he threatens.

I shake my head and reply, "No, she never will." I pull him in, cover his mouth with one hand and sink into him. He struggles, I feel him kick around. None of it matters, he already lost. I take the first gulp, iron and rust flood my insides. I pull back, a sharp breath worsens the already overwhelming taste revealing a harsh chemical aftertaste. Too many drugs!

The flames in my entrails rise to my eyes, the hand anchoring him shifts from his chest to his neck. Like a boa it wraps around him. His eyes bulge turning red, his face purple. He grows limp,

I step back letting him drop to the ground. Nothing but trash. I lick my mouth clean and check myself in the mirror. Shit. I think as I spot a small blood trail on my chest staining my white t-shirt.

Without overthinking it, I slam my nose on the sink. Crack! I look up at my reflection and see my nose fractured and bleeding on my shirt. The pain is high-pitched, it cries like the edge of a razor. I wait for it and like clockwork after every meal, I heal. I wash my hands and rinse my face, then exit the restroom.

"Sorry, I took so long. I blew my nose too hard and ruptured a small vein. Damn thing wouldn't stop, it ruined my shirt. Look," I explain, pointing out the bloodstained shirt.

Kat stares at me and asks, "Jude, are you lying to me?" Her arms cross like a fortress raising its gates. Her eyes peer through me. Shaking my head, I open my mouth and she continues, "I dated a guy with a coke addiction. I want nothing to do with that kind of nightmare." She walks up to me and continues only a couple of inches from my face, "Do I make myself clear?"

"I swear it's nothing like that. Check my pockets," I answer as I turn them inside out.

A few uncomfortable seconds pass before she says, "Fine, but if you're lying, you won't hear the end of it."

We walk for a few blocks, mostly in silence. I can feel my stomach worsen. Lightning fueled cramps twist me from the inside. Doesn't surprise me, the beast is starving, and so am I. Walking alongside Kat is bittersweet. Her scent is delightful, as a man I feel every fiber of my being aching to have her again, but I don't want to rush. Not again, no, I want to take my time with her.

As the monster I have been since the beginning of the twentieth century, Kat is a meal one has to travel to a Michelin-star restaurant in order to eat. She's more than a great meal. She's a life-changing journey of tastes, textures, aromas, and colors. She's an experience. It takes all of me to not devour her here under tonight's beautiful moon. I'm not entirely sure what side of me wants her more.

We stop at a small house, Kat says, "I have a roommate, but she's working nights. You probably won't even see her till late morning tomorrow." She opens the front door and walks in.

I stay put, think carefully, and ask, "So are you sure you want me to come in? I don't want to intrude."

"Do you want to come in or not? I don't know of any guy that has asked me twice. Yes, come in. Keep it up, and I really will think you're a vampire," Kat responds.

I smile and step inside. Nothing is burning. I'm safe. I reassure myself. Kat leads me in and gives me a quick tour. Once in her room, I grab her without warning and hold her. She holds me back and for a moment I feel human again. Her heart beats steadily, I breathe in, taking her scent. Time slows nearly to a halt. Picking her up and placing her in bed, I say, "Thank you for trusting me."

Her only reply is a tender kiss. She pulls me in as she starts to take my clothes off. Everything stops as my shirt covers only my face, and she mumbles, "What happened?"

An expected sigh escapes from my mouth. "Knife scars. It was a long time ago. I rather not talk about it now. Do you mind?" I ask.

Kat removes my shirt saying, "No, of course not. I just didn't notice at the club."

"Do they bother you? You wouldn't be the first," I say.

Her fingers slide across each scar. I can barely feel her exploring me. Her careful touch forces memories to resurface. Memories I wish never happened. My torso is a recovered battlefield. Large and jagged lines drawn on my chest. Short and deep lines are scattered over my abdomen. I'll never forget that night. So much pain, violence, and defiance. It happened ages ago. I'm lucky, that was the last of the wars. Even if it was the worst. Rules were never broken afterwards.

I hear the buttons on my jeans pop open, the zipper next. Her hand wrapping around me brings me out of that unnecessary bloodshed. My eyes open just as her lips reach mine. In what feels like a second, we're exposed and vulnerable. An unspoken agreement between strangers. Trust and pleasure are all we become. The passing of time eventually conquers us. The last thing I see is her face resting on my chest.

My eyes shoot open, a cold sweat covers me. I stay still against my will because I can smell Kat nearby. The clock on her nightstand shows me I've only slept for half an hour. It burns, the hunger my kind bears is maddening. I'm in awe of how similar it feels to a red-hot poker against my skin. A quick turn of my head and I see her face down, her back exposed. The darkness hides nothing from my nocturnal eyes. Every part of her is clear as day to me. Trying to distract myself from the monster's call, I count the freckles on her back. Seventeen, eighteen, nineteen, twen—

"What are you doing?" Kat asks.

"I didn't want to wake you. I'm sorry, I can't sleep," I reply.

Kat turns over to face me. "What's wrong? Is it about the job?"

"No, no. It's ... never mind, go to sleep." I drop back to bed pretending everything is fine.

"No, we agreed on telling the truth. What's up?" she asks as she turns the lights on.

I cover my eyes and confess, "It's my stomach. It won't let me sleep. I'm too hungry."

"Oh my god, Jude. I thought it was something serious. I'm sure there's something in the fridge. Help yourself." The lights turn off and Kat lies back down.

I open my mouth, but from her breathing, I realize she's fast asleep. My eyes are glued to her. I try not to stare so hard as to wake her again. My instincts beg me to eat her. With great effort, I break away. I make my way to the window and see a gray cat strolling in the backyard. Better than that guy. Probably tastes better too. I bet I can get to it, feed, and return without Kat knowing. Yeah, it should hold me a little while. Enough to keep her safe.

A second after convincing myself, I'm slipping out the patio door in her room. The cat's grooming itself, its round paw carefully cleans its face. My footfall is nearly impossible to hear, I take three steps before I stop behind a shrub. I'm careful, the hunt is mostly about how well the plan is executed. I close my eyes and let my other senses take over.

One hundred twenty three, normal heart rate. Smells fine, a little dirty but nothing out of the ordinary. My fangs unsheathe automatically, my nails grow to a point. I slowly open my eyes and see the cat arch, it looks around. As both predator and prey, it senses when a hunt is in progress. My ears pick up my cell phone ringing, I ignore it and wait for my chance.

The lights turn on behind me, the cat runs off and I hear, "What are you doing? Your phone woke me."

A chill rushes over me. I stand up and turn to her, hiding my hands. "I saw a cat and I wanted to pet it," I reply. Her glare cuts me. She knows you're lying dumbass. I step back inside, saying nothing. A stabbing pain shoots through my midsection knocking me down.

"Jude!" Kat screams. She pulls me up, I break free and run to her bathroom. I'm in such a hurry that I slam the door and crack it. The knob starts turning, I press against the door locking it for her safety. "Are you okay? Jude, say something!"

The stabbing pain is suffocating, vengeful, and inopportune. Large breaths buy me time. Time I don't have. This is my final warning. The beast is coming. Heart rate skyrockets, palms sweat, and stomach caves in. I push through this hell saying through ragged breaths, "Stay back. Please. I beg you. It's dangerous. I'm dangerous!"

"What are you talking about? Let me help. I'm calling an ambulance," Kat responds through the door.

The ambulance will only bring unwanted attention. Flexing every muscle in my body to hold it back, I open the door and tell her, "No, no ambulance! I'm leaving. I'm sorry, I should've never come here."

Practically running out the bathroom and to her room, I grab my clothes and head for the front door. The deadbolt becomes an impenetrable puzzle for me. It's nearly impossible to think things through when dealing with the hunger. My claws fumble over and over. Kat catches up with me and reaches out to help. She pulls back gasping as she sees my claws.

I try to speak, to warn her but my voice is gone. Instead, a rabbid snarl comes out. She jumps back and immediately retreats to her room. I cover my mouth and feel my claws on my skin. I take a look at one hand. Darkening gray skin, growing black claws, and the familiar tightening of my body, as my skin thins and stretches to cover the wings sprouting from my back. The sensation grows, it spreads like a tsunami tearing down everything in its path. First my core, then my arms, followed by my back, growing and arching into a shockingly broad expanse.

The pain is unbearable, my legs give out. A loud tearing drowns out my agonizing screams and the rest of the world. I could have prevented this. I lost control while looking for the perfect meal. Now it's here. The thought is seared into my brain. The tightness finally fades away, taking the pain with it. My back feels heavy. I'm on my feet again, a blink later, I'm crashing through the door to Kat's room. At this point, no door can stop me. All I see is a balled-up Kat trapped into a corner. Fear does that to some, shuts them down. Others thrive and get up to fight—not that they ever win. The crackling flap of my wings is the last thing I hear as I black out.

The flavor of pure iron brings me back. Immense pleasure runs through me. Oxygen-filled lungs and adrenaline in my veins make me remember where I am. Kat's mesmerizing scent is embedded in my lips, mouth, and nose. From the savage form of my arms, I know I still hold the form of the beast. That creature that stares back at me in the mirror or any other reflection.

I'm on all fours, trembling, in a puddle of crimson. "Kat?" I utter, incapable of looking for her. I'm in the corner she hid in, it's empty. Where is she? Turning around I see what happened. The bed is riddled with claw marks, walls have blood spatter too. The window is shattered, the glass is mostly gone—presumably outside—signs of an attempted escape. The long white shirt she wore is now torn and completely drenched in red. There's long hair between my fingers; it's black, it's hers.

I call out again, "Kat? Please say something." No reply of course. The chasm in my stomach is vanquished but another in my heart emerges. I don't want to search anymore. I head out and catch my reflection in the hallway mirror. A bat-like monster looks back at me. Savagery and satisfaction fill its yellow eyes. I can't maintain eye contact with it and leave for the beach. It wasn't supposed to be this way. There at the beach, I come to terms with my actions. I drop to my knees, the sand cradles me gently. Her delicious flavor lingers in my mouth. It mocks me, it reminds me of my greatest failure. This is the only remedy. It'll be here in a few seconds. I haven't seen one in so long. There it is. The vibrant orange piercing through the deep blue.

"This morning is a dark one for Santa Monica, there's an ongoing investigation on what can only be described as a heinous act of evil. A young woman, now identified as Kat Montgomery, was found by her roommate torn apart in her home. Authorities have yet to state if there's any relation to another nearby death at the beach where a man was found dead in a public restroom with strange bite marks.

"In a third incident, a charred corpse was discovered by a woman out on her morning run. The body is apparently male, suspected suicide, but the identity is still unknown. Beside it, a note was found with the message, I'm sorry, my love. I hope you can forgive me for what I did. Thank you for reminding me of my humanity.

"Authorities believe this death to be unrelated to the other two."

THE JOURNEY

by Jose Francisco Trevino Chavez

Ba-bump. Ba-bump. Ba-bump. The intense pounding in my chest is audible only to me. The vast ceremonial room lies in complete silence. Everyone stands still in their designated spot. Ten rows of ten people, or as the Hive calls us *prospects*. The white robe hides my shaking knees from everyone.

GONG! GONG! The thunderous crash of the colossal altar gong at the front of the ceremonial room shatters the silence which was holding us still. Everyone's attention turns with a jolt toward the sound. At the altar, he stands tall with his hands raised high, extending toward us. His golden yellow tunic carries the Hive's insignia: a hollow gold pyramid pointing down over an inverted square.

With a single hand movement, his two arch-priests ignite their incense pendulums. The two figures in black robes detailed by a red stripe walk down the altar stairs and over to us. The room fills with scented smoke. As they get closer to the back

I have more difficulty seeing the altar. The smoke infiltrates my nostrils, the mix of aromas is familiar, but I can't pinpoint the individual scents.

The Gold One claps once; his arch-priests stop. He pulls down his hood and says, "Prospects, we have all been given the gift of a worm—a gift from the stars up above—but with these worms comes great responsibility. Tonight each of you will be tested. Your body, mind, and spirit will be pushed to the breaking point. Most of you will break, but the blessed few who succeed will be the first batch in the next evolutionary step of humanity."

GONG! The ceremonial room rumbles again, the Gold One points at one of my oath siblings. His arch-priests immediately go to him and lead him up the altar. He bows toward the Gold One who says, "Rise, my son. If you succeed, it is I who will bow." The young man rises, and the Gold One takes his left arm and asks, "Is your worm awake?"

My oath brother nods and says, "Yes Gold One. It writhes as we speak."

"Wonderful. Do you remember what your worm represents?"

My oath brother nods and says, "It's a physical representation of our shadow."

"Exactly! It seems like you are ready. Let us begin your trial." The Gold One takes the glass bowl off the altar table and hands my oath brother a single black pill. He takes it without hesitation and swallows. The Gold One turns to face us. A few seconds pass, and we all stare at our brother. My left wrist starts to itch, my own worm is getting agitated. I ignore it, I mustn't call attention to myself ... not now. It's his moment, he is the first today. How lucky.

Our brother groans as he grabs his stomach, and his eyes roll back. The Gold One smiles from ear to ear as he raises his arms announcing, "Witness the beginning of a new era!" He steps aside, allowing all of us to focus on our oath brother.

His body twists as he groans louder than before. He falls to his knees, his hands claw at the floor. His mouth opens and black sludge pours out of him. "Please, make it stop!" our oath brother begs, but the Gold One doesn't even acknowledge his pleas. He even steps back, avoiding our brother's hand when it reaches for him.

Our oath brother gasps for air, the sludge continues pouring out from both mouth and nose. I can't keep looking, I lower my eyes and wait for it to end. A few minutes pass, and the awful noises stop. I look up only to see our oath brother frozen in place, his eyes white and mouth wide open. Something moves under his chest. It slithers under his skin. It's his worm, we all have one. It doesn't seem much like a gift at the moment, but the stars gave us the asteroid which held the first worm. We were chosen. It is an honor. At least that's what the Gold One keeps telling us. The ceremonial room is completely silent again. A low rumble starts to echo. It slowly grows.

From his back, it bursts out. *CRUNCH!* A long blood soaked slithering monstrosity slams onto the pristine white granite floor. The crowd gasps with terror, myself included. The Gold One reaches for his waist and draws a gun. *BLAM! BLAM!* The first blast kills the beast, the second, our oath brother. The room fills with the unintelligible mix of frightened voices. Another gunshot goes off, immediately shutting us up.

"Is this not what you expected?" asks the Gold One. "He died because he was weak. Weak of body, mind, spirit, and most importantly, faith! Do any of you wish to return to your safe and mundane life? Speak up. Those who want out, raise your hands."

No one's moving. Silence falls upon us. A hand slowly rises from within the crowd. "You want out? Very well, take a step to your right, prospect."

I can't see them clearly from here, all I see is their head moving. *BLAM!* The Gold One takes a clear shot. The prospect's body falls out of my sight. "This is absolute weakness. Anyone else? No? Good. Time will not be wasted." He looks far into the back of the room. He points in my direction and shouts, "You are the next to take the trial."

Before I can react, I'm being dragged to the front. I stand directly across from the Gold One. His hands stretched out to me, the black pill in his hand waiting. I freeze, my eyes fix on its shiny shell. My hand shakes as I pluck it from his palm. I place it on my tongue and swallow. Everyone's eyes are on me; their stare should fall heavy on my shoulders. I've always had trouble with crowds, yet now ... I'm barely aware of them.

The Gold One has no expression at all, his scarred face and nearly black eyes look into my soul. His eyes dig in like a red-hot branding iron. The itch in my wrist worsens, I can feel the creature wrapping itself around my forearm like a slimy rope sliding between my radius and ulna. I grab my wrist and squeeze it, trying to stop my worm from further separating my bones.

"Do not fight your worm. Embrace it and become one with it. Remember that it is a symbiote, it won't fight you, so why should you?" His words reach me from far away. I try to look up at him, but my eyes roll back. My sight goes black, cold sweat runs down my face, and my knees give out. I feel my worm slither up my arm and around my neck.

My hands shoot to my neck as my worm acts like an internal noose for a seemingly invisible execution by strangulation. I gasp for air, but nothing goes in, and nothing comes out. *Stop, please! I don't want this! Help me! We're supposed to be like family!* Control over my eyes returns, a tasteless victory as my lungs catch fire. All I see is the crowd of white robes staring morbidly as I start to black out. For some unknown reason the phrase: *Face me!* pops into my head just as my eyes close.

My eyes open. All I see is white, slowly my eyes adjust to the glaring brightness. I'm warm. I stand up and look around. Far off in the distance, I see a colossal tower. The grass underneath my bare feet is still covered with morning dew. *How is this possible?* Grass doesn't grow in any of the megacities on Earth. I look up and see the natural blue sky above with a few scattered clouds.

Blue sky? Not gray? I must be hundreds or thousands of miles from any megacity. *Wait, how did I get here? I was...* I gasp from the flash of my last memory. The ceremony. I turn to my wrist expecting to see the bulge of my worm wrapped around it, but there's nothing there. I feel around my arm and neck ... nothing. The itching is gone.

With no one else in sight, I start making my way toward the tower in the distance. A few trees are scattered across the horizon. I take my time walking. The warm weather isn't something to take for granted. The megacities pollute so much that the weather is always cold and damp there. I've only heard about this kind of weather and the descriptions didn't do it justice.

The colors are bright but not over-saturated. The lack of neon lights is unreal to me. *Where are the birds?* There are always at least a few. I continue walking, letting my thoughts flow freely; something thought of as taboo by the Hive. My robe swings along with the light breeze as it tickles my skin. I close my eyes as I walk ahead. I let the sun hug me for the first time in my life. For the first time in almost thirty years, I can walk in peace, no need to hurry.

My laughter breaks the silence, and I cover my mouth until I realize I'm alone. I can't help but smile, and I break out laughing again. All this feels so wrong, the Hive discourages laughter under most circumstances. I feel my abs twitch; joy takes over. I laugh and laugh until my sides hurt. I grab them and try to stop laughing. Eventually, I do. *Focus, get to that tower. You're lost, remember?* With a shake of my head, I clear my mind and continue forward.

Shit, it's far. It'll take ages to get there. Better hurry. I sigh from the irony and start running, but it doesn't feel like I'm getting closer. Eventually I slow down and squint at the tower. It still looks so far away. *How long have I been running?* My thighs start burning. The sun isn't directly above me anymore. It must be around 4 p.m. by now. *Have I been trying to reach the tower since around 7 a.m.?*

I look up and see the clouds gathering in a dark gray mass. *Great, it's going to rain.* I speed up the pace despite my legs protesting with every step. A minute later, the sky takes its first shot. A raindrop hits my face. Then the second, third, and fourth. *Ugh! At this rate, I'll be soaking by the time I reach it. I wish the tower was much closer.*

WHOOSH! My legs give out as a shockwave slams into my chest, it robs the air from my lungs. I see the horizon warp like a rippling pond. The rectangle in the distance grows exponentially in a fraction of a second. It stretches and runs to me. As my body hits the ground, I roll forward, and all I see is a blur of sky, ground, and rain.

I crash against something hard, it stops my rolling. I catch my breath and look up. It's so tall I can't see where it ends. *Is this the tower?* A large pair of black metal doors swing open. I look back to where I was moments ago. *What happened?* I wonder. I stand up and dust my robe off. The sound of a bell coming from behind me catches my attention, before I can turn to it, something pulls me in. The doors slam shut, the bell rings again. *I can't see.*

I slowly walk around in the dense dark, my hands out trying to grab onto anything. I touch what feels like a wall, it's cold and smooth like polished metal. I continue groping blindly until I find a large gap. *Doorway? Feels like one.* I carefully step forward and through the gap. The floor lowers. *A step,* I make my way down the step. *There's another step, no, they're stairs.* I travel down the stairs in what I can only imagine a doubtful toddler looks like.

Sixteen, seventeen, eighteen, nineteen, twenty ... no more? I take two careful steps forward to verify. *No more stairs. Okay, now what? Still can't see.* From an inky black darkness, my eyes are assaulted by fluorescent white lights. The sudden change in lighting forces my eyes shut. I freeze and wait. A few shapes start forming, their colors come next. Then everything comes into focus.

My jaw drops, and I cover my mouth and take a step back. *No, it's not real. Up, down, left, right, upside down? How?* I reel as I try to take it all in. An endless omnidirectional set of brass stairs lies before me. The sharp edges reflect the light in every direction. They look like golden slabs stuck to the walls. I shake my head and turn around. My heart skips a beat. The stairs I used to get here are gone. My palms drip sweat, my mouth dries out, and nausea sets in. My breathing quickens.

I can't breathe, I— WHEEZE! I can't breathe! The nightmare fuel of a room spins. There's pressure growing on my chest. The bell rings again. It clears my mind. *You're hyperventilating! Focus ... you know how!* I purse my lips and breathe through them. The vise around my chest loosens. The room stops spinning as I control myself.

I gather myself and face the paradox before me. It's like Jorge Luis Borges' *THE LIBRARY OF BABEL* or an M. C. Escher piece.

At the center of the room is a tree. Just by looking at it I know it's no ordinary tree. Its robust trunk carries a crown of branches adorned with lush foliage. Each leaf is a vivid green yet it holds every other color known to man. A metal snake slithers around the base of the tree. The golden reptile holds its tail in its maw. *An ouroboros?* If I remember correctly.

Up above the tree hovers a gold orb. It spins ever so slowly. On it is an intricate carving. It consists of ten circles, six arranged in a hexagonal pattern while three are in a triangle pointing down holding the last circle inside it. I know I've seen this diagram before but I don't know where. An old forgotten memory resurfaces. I remember the tattoo my father had on his arm. It was the same as the etching on the orb. He called it the tree of life diagram. I walk up to the tree and reach out to touch it. Just before I reach it, a veil of water falls from the gold orb, as if protecting the tree. Or is it protecting me?

Without any other option, I pick the nearest set of upright stairs and start ascending. The golden sheen of the stairs contrasts wildly with the graphite-colored walls. I climb up and up the stairs, they lead nowhere. Sixty steps up, there's a landing space with a glass showcase.

I take a close look. In the display is a diorama of a boy no older than five. He looks like he's crying as an elderly woman speaks to him. Her expression is tight, worried. There's a plaque that reads, *The Orphan.*

The words slice through me. I step back. My head spins and my heart aches. I can still hear her voice as clearly as on that dreadful day, "I'm sorry child, but you don't need to worry—we'll take care of you here. This orphanage welcomes you with open arms." I let my body go into autopilot and feel as it walks away and climbs further up until I find myself sitting on the next landing for a rest. *Keep going, you need to get out of here,* I tell myself. I stand up, legs shaky and aching.

A voice in my head says, "Look left." My eyes move without permission. Another showcase. Another diorama. It's a ten-year-old boy in uniform. He's facing the wall of a classroom while the teacher strikes him with a stick. His voice is still audible after all this time, "You'll remember this lesson you little monster!" I start to sweat again. My back starts stinging with every lash, flaming predatory tongues abuse my back.

The voice says, "Read the plaque." I do as it says. It reads, *First abuser.*

"No!" I shout to the voice making me look. "Who are you?"

"That's irrelevant. Keep moving," it replies.

I shake my head and say, "I'm not a monster. No, I want to get out. Let me out!" I look back and go down the stairs and take several random turns. Left, down, right, right, left ...

"Are you finished? Where did that tantrum take you?" it asks. "Look at where you are."

Everything looks exactly the same, until I see the first showcase. It's upside down. I turn my gaze up and see the strange tree hanging upside down. Unable to wrap my head around the impossible physics, I continue running. Mindless turns and impulsive decisions are all I have. All I do. All I accept. My body continues this charade of a fruitless attempt to escape. In a furious turn, I miss a step down. Like a thrown die, I tumble down the sharp teeth-like stairs.

The sharp rectangular edges slice at my body with every collision, the world shifts, and the fluorescent lights blind me. All I can do is ball up and hope for survival. My face slams into the cold stone floor. My heart thumps heavily yet far off somewhere. I push myself up and off my face. I grunt as I begin to feel my face again. A wave of pain crashes from my jaw to my nose. A string of drool falls to the ground as I hear the bell ring one more time.

The sound sends shivers down my spine. The high-pitched noise is different from the others. It feels cold, distant, hateful.

"It's awake," the voice announces. I stand up and take the next steps up. I slowly struggle up the steps, my eyes carefully focusing on where my feet land. Eventually, I reach a new showcase. I seem to have landed exactly where the voice wanted me—exactly where I would have landed if I had just kept going. My efforts are futile. Free will begins to seem like an illusion. A trick of the mind.

I hesitate to look into the showcase, yet the urge is stronger than my will. I see a prepubescent boy; he's smoking and drinking. I feel disgusting emotions deep inside me: emptiness, an unwanted misfit, too young for independence, too old for adoption. The taste of cheap liquor washes over my smoke-numbed tongue as though I were back there. I cough and gag, then lower my gaze and read the plaque. It reads, *First escape*. I scoff and continue. "Why? Why show me this? I know the story—I lived it!" I say, expecting an answer.

"Only you know why," the voice replies. "Keep going, finish your journey."

"What journey? I don't know how I got here."

No reply comes. I scratch my wrist. I look around trying to find some sort of exit or door, but all I see are endless stairs. I feel like the more I walk, the less I traverse. Several empty landings pass me by. I'm exhausted. It's endless. *I'll die here, alone. My body will rot and decompose to the bone and no one will ever know.* My grasp on hope loosens, all I can think of is that first showcase. I've been alone since the age of five.

"You are not alone."

"How would you know? I have no family or friends."

"No, I mean here. You are not alone," the voice warns.

"I don't see anyone else. Auditory hallucinations don't count as company—sorry to break it to you."

"Keep going, before it finds you. Before it consumes you," it replies as I sit down. I shake my head. "There are only four more showcases," it explains.

"Look, I don't know what *it,* you are referring to and I don't care. As for the showcases, yeah, I think I understand the pattern now. I'm not moving. I know my life's story. I *hate* it. Don't wanna relive it."

"Please. Do it for us, not just you. You'll lose your persona, your ego, and your true self. We are one," it begs. Its tone carries desperation and fear.

"I said no! What does that even mean? Fuck off!" I shout. The walls bounce my anger back. There's no response.

Alone again, I think. A cynical smirk warps my lips. I know what the other dioramas will be. At sixteen I discovered cutting. Another escape wrapped in self-abuse. The sensation of the blade sliding across my skin comes back to me. That acute pain releases me from my emotional hell. I'm forced to look down at my wrists as the familiar warmth trickles down my arms. *It's not there, that was years ago,* I remember.

With a shake of my head, I continue down memory lane—Arrested at eighteen for grand theft. Police beat me for resisting. My back and sides tense up, their merciless batons slamming against me. I'm barely able to breathe between each strike. In my head, I hear that awful noise again, *CRACK!* I wheeze as I reach for my ribs, their rigidity returns me to reality. *They healed, remember?* I remind myself. *What's this? More abuse, I guess.*

"Of course it's abuse. What else?" I tell myself, covering my face in shame. "Now in my twenties ... I'm trapped inside a pseudo-religious cult," the realization hits like a truck. *This is the last escape.* "Where'd you go?" I ask the voice. "Aren't you going to tell me I'm right?" Only silence accompanies me. I scoff at the lack of an answer. *I'm in a cult.* The mere thought of it brings me to tears. My face is assaulted by a wave of warmth. My jaw tightens, and I can hear the screeching protests coming from my teeth as they grind, remembering all those fake smiles and empty promises. They approached me in prison, I was an easy prey. I was at my lowest. They nurtured me and waited for me to lower my guard. *It's my fault. I'm responsible for this.*

I break down. My own body heat becomes an inferno. Tears and sweat become indistinguishable from one another. A primal scream pours out of me leaving me drooling and tired. With my mind clear, it dawns on me. "Wait a minute, that's only three showcases. What's the last one?" I grab my wrist as it starts burning. I look down and my blood chills. A black venous stain presents itself where the itch used to be, where the mark of my worm was. I wipe it with my sleeve, but nothing happens.

It's underneath my skin! Is my worm still in me? The thought sends shivers through me. My confusion sends my mind into a downward spiral again. The solitude weighs me down, the air thins out. I scurry to my feet and search my body again. The voice said I wasn't alone. *Now, where are you?* I ask both my worm and myself. My hands travel around my body, they grope every part possible. Arms, legs, neck, back, and torso. Nothing.

An intense piercing heat running through my wrist brings me to my knees. I look down and see the stain is mostly gone. In its place is a fresh gaping wound. A small amount of blood runs down my arm. I hear a wet slithering sound at my feet. I turn to the sound and catch a glimpse of something gray escaping under nearby stairs. I freeze for a second. Fighting back a shudder. I make my way to it.

The lights go off. I stop immediately. *Shit! What now?* I can't see a thing. A deep hellish tolling bell roars throughout the solid darkness. The stone floor shakes, and I struggle to stay upright. Then a heavy silence falls around me. I focus on any possible sound. The strong sound of my heart is the only sound I hear. *Ba-bump! Ba-bump! Ba-bump!*

The passing of time eludes me, and I don't know how long I've been in complete darkness. A wet thud coming from behind me catches my attention. I turn around and hear something sloshy dragging along the ground near me. I kneel down and tentatively grope at the cold floor—wanting to find the source and simultaneously not wanting to. The noise stops as my hand reaches out. All I hear is my shallow breath. *Come on eyes, adjust already!*

The darkness is too thick. I continue feeling blindly with my hands. I hear it again, then it slides up to me from the right. I turn and reach for it and my fingers collide with a thick film. I pull back and feel the viscous residue clinging to my fingers. It's cold, like the floor. I feel small debris stuck to it. Then, a distance away, I notice something.

I squint, forcing my eyes to focus. Between the ocean of darkness, I notice a pair of white dots. *Light!* I reach up to rub my eyes—make sure they're clear—and a dreadful stench of sulfur and rotting fish invades my nostrils. *Ugh!* I gag. I pull my contaminated hands away.

The lights are still there, in the distance. They blink twice. I slowly move toward them and they blink again. They slide away to the side, then I hear a low rumbling chuckle. They're eyes! I see them rise up well above my head. I scurry backwards, an awkward crablike crawl, so I can keep my eyes on the creature.

"I told you you weren't alone," the voice says. I pay little attention to it. I crash against a set of stairs, unable to see my surroundings and unable to move, I fall back on something I have always loathed. *Prayer.*

I start murmuring the only prayer I still remember from that abusive orphanage. "Our Father, Who art in heaven, hallowed be Thy name. Thy kingdom come. Thy will be done on earth as it is in heaven. Give us this day our daily bread and forgive us our trespasses as we forgive those who trespass against us, and lead us not into temptation, but deliver us from evil."

The bright white eyes get bigger as they get closer and closer. The darkness is lit up for a split second, and I take in its shape—a long gray featureless thing staring at me—before the flash of light disappears, leaving only its white eyes visible again, piercing through me. I slide left and try to crawl backwards. The light flashes on and off like a twisted nightclub. Each flash reveals more of the hidden thing.

I see it sliding my way. The oozing gray skin and snakelike body is no more. In a flash I see stumps forming. In another, I get a glimpse of arms and legs as it crawls closer to me. I feel it grabbing my leg, I pull away, but it's useless to fight; it's too strong. It pulls me close to it, and I feel its clawed digits wrapping around my limbs. It straddles me, and stares into my eyes as it sits on my chest.

I feel the creature's heavy breathing on me. The awful stench from before returns much stronger now. A warm sensation spreads across my face. The light flashes, revealing the now mostly human creature drooling on me. It locks eyes with mine and when darkness covers us again it says, "Submit."

My body twists without my consent, my arms push against the thing's grip. It roars in my face. The crooked sound itches against my bones. I see an opening and take it. I lunge my head forward and bite down on its ear. I feel its cartilage give as it crunches against my teeth. My bite severs a vein, warm blood gushes into my mouth. Iron, salt, and rotting fish are all I taste.

The creature breaks free from my mouth and retreats. Its heavy footfall bounces off every surface. The darkness is no longer its weapon but its protector. I stand and shout, "Fight me, bitch!" I see the white eyes bobbing around as they get smaller and smaller. I ask myself, *What are you doing? Don't challenge it, run!* The fragment of courage in me wavers as I start looking around for something, anything that can help me get away. The flashes continue, lighting parts of my space.

I walk aimlessly through the intermittent darkness, constantly checking for the thing's eyes. A yellow line of light appears in the opposite direction of the thing. It looks like a small gap between doors. I bolt to it, every step sends a tingling protest down my legs. I've been walking around for who knows how long, my legs need to rest, but I ignore their pleas.

Every so often I turn around and look for those eyes. Still there. The line gets brighter with each step I take, the eyes get smaller too. The intermittent flashing stops. An invisible fire burns at my legs, I know it's not real, it's exhaustion. *Keep running!* Every step becomes heavier than the last. Now it feels like I'm running through molasses. Sweaty, panting, and sore, I look behind me.

My eyes sweep through the darkness, left, right, nothing. *Where is it?* The thought repeats itself over and over as I walk backwards. The wall stops me from moving. I feel blindly behind me and find the gap and slide my fingers through it. *I have to turn around, get through this door.* I hesitate to act. *No! That thing will attack me.*

The voice returns saying, "You have to."

"I know but—"

"But nothing!" it replies. I know it's right. I take a deep breath and turn around. My fingers fit perfectly into the gap. I pull left and right as I try to slide the door open. It's heavy, I keep pulling until I feel a slight budge from the door. It starts sliding left. I put all of my weight into it. I feel it sliding a bit more. The door slides open enough for my arm to slip through. I try a different grip, it opens further.

A few drops of sweat fall to my hands. I wipe them off and then wipe my face only to find it dry. Two more drops, this time on my head. I look up and, in the ocean of black, two white dots are staring down at me. The thing drops on me knocking me down. It claws at me. My chest burns with every swipe. I kick and punch in the dark. The only source of light is the partially open door, my sole escape route.

The yellow light falls on the creature as it moves frantically through its attack. I see it now has a human face. Slim jawline, long black hair, and those eyes. Those unholy white eyes. As it's attacking me, I feel it drooling on me. A sharp knifelike pain drags through my chest and into it. I can't breathe. *I'm going to die. I'm dying!* That's all I can think about.

I grasp at it. My hand lands on the thing's neck. I wrap my hand around it and squeeze as much as possible. I dig my nails into its oozing skin. The thunderous cry from both fury and pain hurts my ears, but I don't stop. The cold ooze runs down my hand and, suddenly, I feel it turn warm. *I broke skin!* I tell myself as I try to stay conscious.

I feel its blood pooling on my chest. I dig further in and try to *see* with my fingers what I'm touching. A throbbing sensation catches my attention, I waste no time and yank it with every bit of strength in me. The roar is interrupted by a bubbling gurgle. The creature stops clawing at me and grabs its neck at an attempt to stop the bleeding. It falls to its side, writhing.

I struggle to stand and make my way through the gap. I ignore the gashes on my chest and continue onward. To my surprise, all I see is a long and brightly lit hallway. I continue forward as I see a tall rectangle at the end. *Is it a door? An exit?* Every stumbling step forward gives me hope. I lean on the wall as I walk. I'm breathing heavily, I'm dizzy, and I feel blood flowing down my chest.

I stop, staring in shock. Standing across from me is the creature. I slowly turn around to take a look. At the beginning of the hall I can see the gap I came in from hasn't changed. I turn back and take a step forward, and so does the creature. Our eyes lock, two badly wounded beings full of hate, bloody and dying.

With great effort, I take the deepest breath possible and stand as straight as my body allows. I shout, "You don't scare me anymore. Come on! Let's see who wins!" The creature says the same thing. At the same time. My chest deflates, my heart sinks as the cold realization hits me. I take the last steps forward and reach out. Our hands touch. My reflection. Tears run down my face. In the mirror I see a plaque just like the ones on the showcases. It reads, *Completion*.

"No. No! NOOOO!" I scream. I punch my reflection over and over. *I'm not a monster. I'm not! Am I?* I fall to my knees and close my glowing white eyes. I hear myself laughing, but I hear it far away. I want to go back home, wherever that is. *Please.* The bell rings again as I faint.

The violent sensation of cold air filling my lungs forces my eyes open. I look up and see my oathsiblings. Their eyes wide and full of terror, their hands covering their mouths. I stand up, the colors seem brighter, the aromas of the incense pendulums the arch-priests carry jump out to me. I breathe in—juniper, myrrh, and sandalwood, my nose tells me.

"Yes, my son! You are strong in mind, body, spirit, and faith!" The Gold One shouts. I turn to him and see him smiling from ear to ear.

My head tilts. *Is he referring to me? He is.* I smile and return my attention to the Gold One. His right hand stretches over to me. I gently take it and notice my gray skin. The touching of our hands causes my eyes to shift. Everything turns gray except for the people who are now pulsating a bright red.

I can see his heart. His blood vessels too. My eyes wander throughout his entire body. Hypocrite! He doesn't have a worm! *Don't overthink it. Do it*, I tell myself. "Were you ever going to tell us?" I ask the Gold One.

His eyes blink rapidly. He forces a smile and replies, "Tell you what?"

I squeeze my hand as hard as possible. *CRUNCH!* The bones in his hand feel like brittle twigs as they snap from the pressure. He screams as his knees betray him, sending him to the ground. His screams make me salivate. *BLAM! BLAM! BLAM!* Three consecutive crackles of thunder steal my attention. I feel a light trickle running down the back of my head. I touch it, it's healing instantly. My skin feels thick and hard like a suit of armor or an exoskeleton.

I'm greeted by the smoking barrel of a pistol as I turn around. One of the two arch-priests is holding it. The other ... I can't see. I don't care about him. I reach for the gun, my speed is unnatural, unmatched. I swipe it away and grab his neck. He collapses like cardboard, twisting around like a leech.

I return to the Gold One. *He's afraid.* His heartbeat is skyrocketing. I turn to the paralyzed crowd and say, "He has no worm in him! He lies! I won't follow a hypocrite! Will you?"

The crowd says nothing. They only murmur in fear.

I look at the crowd and close my eyes. Something in me shifts again. "I will not treat you like him. Those of you who wish to leave, raise your hands," I tell the crowd in an odd double voice. The crowd hesitates briefly, then a brave woman raises her hand, a few more follow. "No one will have a worm. Forced evolution is dangerous."

I begin chirping at an increasingly high frequency. The people start vomiting. Soon after, their worms are expulsed from their bodies, withering away immediately. "You may leave," I tell the brave people who raised their hands. Once they do, about three-quarters remain. I stare at them for a second. "Those of you who remain, I thank you. Know that you are free to leave at any time," I announce. I turn to the Gold One and say, "This is how you gain a following. Through respect, not intimidation."

"Mercy! Please, I beg of you!" the Gold One tells me.

"You will be repaid with the coin you use," I reply. I take his head and squeeze. It cracks like an egg under pressure. I look down to the granite floor and catch my reflection. I have become the creature. My shadow and I have merged into one.

DINNER FOR TWO

by Jose Francisco Trevino Chavez

The serene melody of "Virginia Moon" by Foo Fighters plays on vinyl, filling the Holguín family dining room. The table is set and dressed—white linen, candles, and a single rose adorn it. A man with light brown hair and gentle melancholic eyes places a small basket of bread on the table before returning to the kitchen. A woman sits silently.

From inside the kitchen, he says, "Dinner is almost ready, sweetheart. I'm just waiting for the cheese to bubble." No more than two minutes later, he returns and places two small bowls of French onion soup on the table. He sits down across from her. "I know things have been rough lately, but I want tonight to be our little pristine moment. Let's just pretend that none of this ..." He takes a deep breath. "Lucy, you're my wife—no matter what—" he starts to tear up, but forces a smile. "And we'll enjoy our ninth anniversary." He wipes his eyes and continues, "Sorry, you know how emotional I am. Enough of that, I hope you enjoy the food. It's vegetarian, just the way you ... well ... the way you *used* to like it."

He plunges his spoon into the bowl of soup. The bubbling cheese stretches from the pressure, steam escapes from the elastic prison releasing the sweet aroma of caramelized onions. He takes it in, his mouth waters. A sad smile forms on his face, he looks into her hazel eyes and tells her, "You look beautiful tonight, even though ... I mean, despite ..." he buries his face in his hands so she can't see her own reflection in his eyes. Taking another deep breath, he looks up again. "I don't know if I ever told you this, but from the moment I saw you, I knew you were the one. I know, I know—it sounds so corny, but it's true." He takes the last two spoonfuls of soup and continues, "It's funny, I ... no, I shouldn't tell you." He glances up at the blank look in her eyes. "Oh, you want me to tell you? Okay. I had seen you before Dave's party. In fact, I saw you about six months before we met."

He stands up and picks up his bowl, he reaches for hers and stops, he stares at the bowl and asks, "Babe, what's wrong? You haven't touched your soup. Did you not like it?" His dark brown eyes return to her hazel eyes. Lucy says nothing, a second turns to ten awkward seconds, and "Virginia Moon" ends, leaving the vinyl player silent. He smiles nervously at Lucy and says, "Boy, am I an idiot or what? You're tied to your chair. Let me feed you, I'm sorry, you must be starving."

He gently removes the cloth gag around her mouth, careful not to get his fingers too close to her teeth. She opens her mouth and slowly moves her jaw up and down, her movements clumsy, fatigued. He pretends not to notice the reddened, swollen, and cracked skin that used to be so soft. Or the eyes that once sparkled, now bloodshot and fixed on the spoon.

"You'd like some, I can tell," he says gently. His voice cracking a little, broken, as he grabs the bowl and spoon-feeds her. He smiles softly and says, "It's good, right?"

Lucy stares at him silently, she swallows the last spoonful and tries to speak, but only a raspy grunt emerges. He can almost imagine her silky voice as it once was. He carefully wipes her mouth clean with a cloth napkin then says, "Don't wear yourself out, sweetie. I'll get the main course now." He stands up and reaches for the bowls, then turns back and walks to the vinyl player. His fingers jump from record to record as his lips mouth their titles. He stops and pulls out his choice. The record spins, the needle latches to the groove, and Café Tacvba's "Eres" starts playing.

Lucy's eyes shoot toward the record player. He takes notice and kneels next to her. "You remember? Remember the day you first heard this song? I do ... I think you do too. It was then that I had planned on proposing to you. I would've too if my car hadn't broken down. Anyway, I'll be right back." He walks away from Lucy and into the kitchen. He can hear the frantic scratching as fingernails dig into the wooden armrests. He's confident that the duct tape around her wrists and ankles will hold tight, but he glances into the room just the same. *She's getting hungry. I better get her some meat.*

When Lucy hears him walking back to her, her mouth opens and with great effort, she tries to speak. Again only gravel-like grunts emerge. Her blank eyes give no clue as to what she wants.

"I'm here, don't worry. I won't leave you, *ever*." He places a silver tray on the table. "I made beef Wellington." He pours two glasses of red wine and pulls out a large knife. It slices through the perfectly cooked dish like a hot knife through butter. He places the pastry-covered medallion, followed by a side of balsamic Brussels sprouts, on the plate. He lovingly cuts a bite-sized piece and carefully brings the fork to her lips, paying special attention to where his fingers are. Her teeth clamp down hard, clanging on the fork. Jumping back, he says, "Easy there, don't hurt yourself ... or me."

Lucy devours her meal, but her movements are slow, stiff—mechanical. When they finish, he grabs her hand gently, careful not to cringe at the feel of her cold skin. His eyes lower, the forced smile he wore seconds before is nowhere to be seen. Her fingers try reaching his hand, the sharp fingernails aiming for his flesh, but he's careful to keep his hand over hers. *Must not let her grab me.*

"I wish things had gone differently. I know it sounds like I'm ... *crazy*? Yes, that's what anyone would say, but they aren't in my shoes. I hate having to do this to you. To me. To *us*." He places his hands behind his head as if holding his head in place. He frowns, his face twisting painfully. "I vowed to be by your side through thick and thin. In wealth and poverty. In health and sickness. That's what I'm doing, damnit!" His hand slams against the table knocking down his glass of wine. Lucy jumps from the impact. "Oh, sweetie, I don't want to scare you. I'm sorry, it's just that Hannah keeps popping into my head. She told me that I had to let you go. Can you believe her? She mentioned she did that when her perfect husband Mark got ...

sick. Like you. Did you notice he's not around anymore? He left. She let him—to protect herself."

He starts wiping the wine off the table as best as he can. He drinks directly from the bottle and says, "She knew what had happened to you. She knew that I would never let you go, but how could I? We argued about it, and then she heard you groaning and banging around down in the basement. 'Is that Lucy down there?' she challenged me.

"I didn't answer.

"'Say something, Roberto!' she hollered. Well ... you probably heard it all, didn't you?" His voice lowers as he says, "I didn't deny it. I couldn't. She hit me and ran down to try to free you. Foolish. You'd never be free that way, there's only one way to free you from this. So I did what anyone else would."

Roberto looks at Lucy, her mouth open and eyes tearing up. He shouts as he points at her, his jaw clenched and neck tightening, "Don't look at me like that Lucy! I had to kill her! She had gotten to you and you ... you *bit* her." Roberto covers his face with his hands. "You know what that means." Through stifled sobs, he softly tells Lucy, "Why didn't she just mind her own business? I didn't want to kill her! But it was too late for her. Can you even understand what I'm saying? She was going to end up just like you. Look at yourself—no don't."

Through shaking hands, he stares at her. His glare is hot enough to melt metal, his breathing is heavy, erratic. Roberto stops shaking, his body heats up and from deep within, it bursts out. He throws the wine bottle across the dining room, it shatters on impact. *I— I can't do this anymore.*

FEAR

He walks over to his room and goes to his safe hidden in the closet. His shaking fingers make it nearly impossible to get the combination right. He breathes deeply to calm down, his mind slows down and he manages to open the safe. As he exits their room, he sees their wedding photo on the dresser. He stares at her beautiful smile until a guttural moan escapes from somewhere deep inside him. He turns the picture face down and keeps moving. His eyes are red and tearing, carrying nothing but despair and the one thing that will bring them both peace. He enters the dining room and stares at Lucy, trying to see the vivid, joyful, and curious woman that was in the wedding photo. It doesn't work; only a palid, worn out, and decaying shell of a woman remains. Her gaze is miles away. *Hannah was right. It's not my Lucy anymore.*

He softly strokes Lucy's face. His touch triggers a snap reaction from her. Roberto knew this was coming, he barely dodges her teeth as she tries one last time to bite. He snaps his fingers to get her attention, she looks up at him. "You know this is the only way," he tells her, "I'm not sure if I did this out of love, denial, or desperation. What I do know is that I love you. What I'm about to do, I do it out of mercy. Is that mercy for you or me? I still don't know. I might never know."

Roberto leans in and kisses Lucy's forehead. He brings his hand up to her and says in a broken voice, "I hope to see you on the other side. I'll always love you, Lucy." He looks away. *CLICK.* His hand shakes, and all he hears is the incessant *CHOMP, CHOMP, CHOMP!* of her attempts at biting him. *But what does it matter now?* He rolls his sleeve and looks away while bringing his left forearm up to Lucy allowing her teeth to sink in. As she goes for the second bite ... *BANG!* His heart sinks, there's no going back now. There's only one way out, *BANG!* His body falls into her lap. Roberto wears his first genuine smile of the evening.

Dead Tongues

DEAD TONGUES

by Jose Francisco Trevino Chavez

"Pizza delivery," a calm voice says through the door on room 243 after knocking.

The door opens, and a young lady wrapped in a towel lets the man inside. "Please leave the food on the bed."

"Sure thing," he replies. He closes the door, follows her instructions, and as she hands him his tip, he says, "Excuse me miss ... I'm sorry, I didn't get your name. This is for Lucy Ricci. Please tell me that's your name. I messed up the last three deliveries."

"It's me."

A sigh of relief escapes from his mouth, and he takes the tip. He stands still staring at her. "Are you familiar with the story of St. Lucy?"

"No, why?"

The man shakes his head and replies, "I am." He sucker punches her. The impact knocks her down, and her head bounces off the carpet. The impact leaves her dazed. Her eyes wander around, her arms barely move. He crouches and mounts her. He brushes her long blonde hair off her face.

A light groan leaves her mouth as two more punches strike her jaw. The numbness runs away from her as a loud crack accompanies a ferocious pain. Her jaw falls open.

"Shh. Don't tire yourself," he says.

His hand wraps around her dainty neck, which starts progressively squeezing. Her arms latch on to his hand, she fights his iron grip. From his back pocket he pulls out something. *SCHWING!* Her eyes widen as she catches her reflection in his blade.

His words still echo in my head: "Follow protocol, Steve. Remember that your *kind* is still under a trial run. Think of it as probation." *I'm glad, he's smarter than most* non-casters. A smirk sneaks onto Steve's cold face.

The cab he's on halts to a stop. "We're here, that'll be $27.42. Card, cash, or phone?" says the driver.

"Phone. Where's your scanner?" Steve answers. The driver's large hand reaches back pointing at the scanner. After paying, Steve opens the cab's door and plants his boot in a muddy brown puddle. The ripples distort the damp gray clouds caught in the reflection. Steve looks up and sees four patrol cars illegally parked by the entrance of his destination, a rundown hotel. *Time's corrosive touch really fucked you up, hasn't it? Poor thing. Me too, me too.*

He makes his way inside and heads straight to room 243 via the elevator. Steve covers his nose trying not to cough from the countless decades of cigarette smoke still lingering inside.

DING! The elevator chimes as its doors open. With one foot still in the elevator, a man's voice warns, "This floor is off limits. It's an active crime scene."

Steve replies, stepping out, "I know. I'm the specialist officer Olivares recommended." He shows the officer his I.D.

"Alright Mr. Norton, this way," the officer replies, leading Steve directly to the crime scene. Before entering, the officer stops him to warn, "Body's been there a while. You'll want to cover your nose or something."

He nods and enters. Three pairs of eyes land on him. From a large mirror in the back of the room, a bouncing camera flash blinds him. The door closes behind him as his eyes shut. "You Norton?" a gruff voice asks.

"Yeah. You must be ..." Steve holds his breath and reaches for the cinnamon gum in his back pocket. He counts his chews, *Seven, eight, nine, ten.* Exhaling through his nose and quickly inhaling through his mouth, an electrically charged wave of cinnamon crackles across his tongue. A pleasant distraction from the fetid stench of humid decay contaminating the air. "That long, huh?"

"What?" The voice asks.

"I mean the victim," Steve replies, opening his eyes and seeing the person attached to the voice. A wide square of a man with stubble and a receding hairline. "Judging from the smell, they've been dead for weeks," Steve explains while shaking hands with him.

"Yes, we believe three weeks. I'm Detective Roberts. Olivares speaks highly of you, I hope he's right. Forensics are finishing up. As soon as they are, you can take a look."

Steve leans on the wall and says, "I've got time. I don't work multiple cases at once. Afterwards I have to decompress." After clearing his throat, he continues, "Olivares here?"

"I'm here," a thin man with a deep black trimmed beard calls out as he carefully traverses the room avoiding the forensic team. "Glad you took the job. Nervous?"

"Why would I be? It's a corpse not a monster. Besides, I'm only going to have a quick chat," Steve replies.

"You're up, Norton," says Detective Roberts.

Steve takes a second stick of gum, "Either of you want gum?" Both decline. "Alright, I need the room. Please close the door on your way out."

"Over my dead body," Roberts protests. "You aren't in charge here. I am."

Steve turns to Olivares in complete silence. Olivares sighs and tells Roberts, "Take it easy, sir. Look, remember how I warned you he was odd? Well this is it. It's his ... *protocol* is it?"

"Call it whatever you like, either accept my terms or I walk. Your choice." Steve's warning comes without even looking at Roberts.

Through gritted teeth and a jaw so tight it might as well be wired shut, he says, "Fine but only because Olivares trusts you. Move anything or contaminate my scene, and I'll have your ass hanging on my office wall."

"I never do."

As soon as they leave, he places a small metal door jam and locks the door. From his jacket's pocket he pulls out a box of chalk. Above the door and the only window available, he draws a *theta nigrum*.

He makes his way to the bathroom ignoring the body on the bed and stares at his reflection. A heavy sigh emerges from him after seeing his weathered face. *Congrats, Steve, you look fifty-something despite your ID claiming forty two. Look at your hair; mostly white. At least the beard is mostly black. After this job's over you go on vacation. Now quit stalling.*

Steve clears his mind and walks over to the bed where the body is. The acrid stench annihilates all traces of his extra strength cinnamon gum. Splayed over the bed, naked and face up, there she rests. Just looking at her lights a torch in Steve's stomach. Her face is badly beaten, jaw obviously broken and crooked. *She took a hate-fueled beating.* On her belly rests a tray, her eyes have been gouged out and on display. She's positioned in a way that makes it look like she's holding the tray in place. One would think so too, if it weren't for her severed head beside her.

His crimson-brown eyes tear up, he wipes them with his sleeve and crouches next to what he knows used to be a healthy young woman. *Let's have a chat, sweetheart. Help me find this monster.* His hand hovers over her. His lips moving in silence. He takes a deep breath and holds it.

He snaps his fingers and waits. The silence is broken by a slow exhale. "Why am I here? I—I was in—"

"I know, sweetheart. My name is Steve Norton, I'm here for a quick chat. Can you tell me your name?"

"What? No, I want to go back."

Pinching the top of his nose, Steve replies, "I know, sweetie. What's your name? I need you to focus."

"Lucy. My name is Lucy."

"What's the last thing you remember?"

"I remember pain, a lot of it."

"Can you tell me why? Tell me everything you can."

"I, um, I wasn't alone," Lucy moans lightly, and Steve hears her discomfort. "He hit me. No reason why." Lucy begins to breathe heavily, her voice wavers like that of a frightened child, "We were talking."

"About what? Can you remember?" Steve leans forward wanting to get every word.

"I'm not sure. I wasn't paying attention."

Steve knows time has run out, his mouth starts tasting iron. He touches the inside of his cheek and sees his finger. *Blood. Great, just great.* "Thank you Lucy, I'll let you go now," he waves his hands over her head. His fingers are bent halfway except for his index fingers. He turns his palms up and hears Lucy exhale. He quickly covers his nose with his hand, catching the blood before it hits the floor.

"I'll find him. I promise," Steve stands and is met with a powerful dizzy spell. He grasps at the wall barely able to stay upright. An angry knocking on the door forces Steve to stabilize himself.

"What's taking him? I'm getting him out," Detective Roberts tells Olivares. His meaty fist pounds on the door.

"No, wait! Sir please, let him do his thing," Olivares says, trying to calm Detective Roberts.

"Shut up Olivares, he's had enough time," grabbing the doorknob, his hand twists and turns, but the door doesn't budge. He tries again and again. It's no use.

A few seconds later the door opens. "I'm finished. Thanks for your patience," Steve says to Detective Roberts. He walks up to him and continues as he finishes wiping his nose, "Interrupt me again and I walk. Now if you'll excuse me, gentlemen, I have to go over what I learned from Lucy and read the report. The guy we're looking for—he's no amateur."

Steve starts walking, Detective Roberts follows, "How do you know the victim's name?"

Steve shrugs.

He's pulled back as Detective Roberts snaps, "No! Quit your coi attitude. Explain! Why do you assume it's a he?"

"She told me her name. Is that what you wanted to hear? Of course not, I asked an officer. As for the gender, most murders are committed by men. Happy?" Steve removes Roberts' hand off himself and leaves.

―――ele―――

After a cab ride to the precinct, Steve sits on a folding chair. The old metal complains under Steve's weight. In his hands lies the folder containing the official report. He skims through it, *This is it? Besides her name and what he did to her, there's nothing else.*

Not even a trace of the killer. No prints, hair, nothing. He tosses it aside, sighing. He sits there motionless for a while, he lets his mind wander.

Finally, he stands up and finds one of the officers. "Hey, mind if I take a look through the unsolved murders?"

"Can't. Detective Roberts warned us not to give you access without his permission."

"Thanks," Steve walks off. He gets his phone out and starts going down the list of his contacts. *Olivares, Olivares, there you are.* Just before his finger taps on the name, a bubbling rumble coming from his stomach gets Steve's attention. He looks at the time. It's getting late and he realizes he's had nothing to eat all day and even skipped breakfast. *Fine. I'll eat.* Steve decides to call later.

"Cheeseburger with a side of fries for the handsome man lost in his thoughts," a beautiful smiling brunette waitress in her forties says loudly, snapping Steve out of his head.

The silence of his mind shatters, letting through the lively chatter of people and ambient music. He looks up and smiles, "Thank you, I'm starving. And more importantly, thanks for the white lie."

"Is my nose growing?" her brows scrunch as she points to her small feline nose.

Steve shakes his head.

"That's right, my mother didn't raise a liar."

Steve nods. "Point taken. Well thank you for the compliment. Especially coming from a woman that has turned several heads since I've been here."

"Now who's lying?"

Steve takes a fry and says between bites, "The teen at table eight keeps staring at your butt. The two old men in the corner booth said you look like a mix between Elisabeth Taylor and Audrie Hepburn. There's a bald guy sitting alone by the jukebox, which I assume is just for show. His eyes have been glued to you ever since you walked by. I can keep going. I don't blame them for looking, but discretion is the name of the game. Otherwise it's creepy."

Wide eyed, embarrassed, and blushing, she responds, "Did you look?"

"I noticed. I have to agree with the old men, their description of you is spot on. You are very attractive."

She smiles and points at the vacant chair across Steve, he nods welcoming her company. "So what are you thinking so hard about? No, sorry. I'm overstepping."

"It's fine. Work. I'm a freelance investigator. I'm looking for an absolute monster."

"Oh gosh. What did he do?"

Steve zips his lips, shaking his head. He takes the first bite of his cheeseburger. The beef's flavor bursts through followed by the cool tomatoes and crunchy onions. The melted cheese creates a soft undertone tying everything together with the subtle sweetness of the brioche bun. He wipes his mouth, smiles, and says, "Can't say more. I have to follow protocol. Sorry. I'm Steve, by the way."

She nods, "I understand. My name's Cecilia, but everyone calls me Cece. From your smile, I take it you like the burger."

"Love it, Cece. Thank you."

"We'll, I'm glad. I have to return to work now. I hope you figure out whatever it is you need." She stands up and walks away. Leaving Steve to his meal.

A man stands by the side of the road, he has his hand out for every passing vehicle to see. He's standing by his car, it was his grandfather's, it stalled for the fifth time this month. He checks his phone. The screen won't respond, "No, don't die now!" The last few rays of sunlight faded away hours ago. He spots a car coming his way. It slows down, ultimately stopping right next to the man.

The window rolls down, and a voice says, "Can I help you?"

"Oh, thank you. Yes, I texted a friend but my phone's dead, so I don't know if he responded," he explains.

"Get in," says the driver.

The man gets in the car, they shake hands and drive, "Thank you so much. You don't have to take me home. My friend works at a bar downtown, it's closer."

The driver nods and says, "You're the boss ... I didn't catch your name. I'm Andrew."

"Lawrence, a pleasure."

The driver, who's been smiling the whole time, wipes his smile away with his hand. Taking a deep breath, he grips the steering wheel until his knuckles turn snow-white. He looks through his rear-view mirror and nods as if getting permission from someone. His smile returns. A little while later, he says, "Do you mind if I check my trunk for something?"

"No, not really."

Andrew parks his car and goes to his trunk. He opens it and grabs what he's looking for. He returns to the driver's seat asking, "I'm curious Lawrence, do you know how St. Lawrence became a martyr?"

Lawrence turns to him, he scratches his head saying, "No, not really. I should, I was raised Catholic. Why do you ask?"

Andrew raises his hand and presses down on the pepper spray can he's holding. The spray hits Lawrence directly in the eyes. He screams covering his face. Blinded, he reaches for the door. Andrew pulls him back by the hair. Lawrence flails his arms but misses every strike. Andrew begins pummeling him with the can's bottom on the head. A few strikes later, Lawrence goes limp.

Andrew wipes the blood off his face and drags Lawrence out of the car into the middle of the road. Lawrence moves slightly, he groans before getting the wind knocked out of him from a powerful kick. Andrew returns to the trunk of his car and returns with a canister of gasoline and drenches Lawrence from head to toe. He turns Lawrence face up and forces him to drink some. Andrew steps back and tosses a lit lighter Lawrence's way.

RING, RING, RING! The obnoxiously loud ringtone on Steve's phone wakes him. His hand clumsily fondles his nightstand. His eyelids refuse to open, so he answers blindly, "What?"

"Sorry, man, I know it's late, but we really need you to help us," Olivares explains.

Steve takes a second to let himself process what's happening. He barely manages to open his eyes and mumbles, "Huh? I am helping."

"No, a different case."

"I only work one case at a time. You know this and you know why," Steve hangs up and tosses his phone aside.

RING, RING, RING! His phone demands attention again. *Why?* Steve picks up the phone and shouts into it, "I'm going to kill you, Olivares! What?!"

"I know, I know. This is weird, man. Like your type of weird. I wouldn't have called if it wasn't important. I'll send you my location."

Steve sighs and knows Olivares is right. *Ever since I told him, he's never given me a regular case. Just odd ones.* Steve takes a look at his phone and sees the text showing Olivares' location. He arrives at the location via taxi half an hour later. Three patrol cars block the road; they paint the night sky in red and blue flashes. Near the patrol cars is a single ambulance and a fire truck.

Olivares waves at Steve and lets him through the yellow police tape, "Hey, man. Long story short, a guy was beaten and burned alive about an hour ago. The thing that made me call you—a woman was driving by, she saw someone fleeing the scene. She recorded it with her phone. Take a look."

Steve takes the phone and plays the video. The camera focuses on a bright orange fire, something in the fire is moving. The camera then focuses further back, something is moving fast. The camera tries to focus over and over, but it simply can't. The only thing visible is a black blotchy stain. Steve's eyes widen, he feels the familiar insect-like crawl of his neck hair standing. He turns around and immediately searches out the woman. She's in the ambulance, shaking and sobbing.

Steve bolts over to her, he shoves the phone in her face and asks, "When you filmed, could you see this thing or did you see a person?"

"Sir, please step aside—" a paramedic begins telling Steve, but he's not having it.

Steve shoves him aside and snaps, "Fuck you!" Returning to the woman, he insists, "Well? Answer me!" Steve's become so frantic that spittle flies off his mouth.

The woman stares at him for a good second before nodding, "I saw a person."

"FUCK!" Forgetting his surroundings, Steve lets out a growling scream as he kicks and punches the air around him.

Three officers surround him, one tries to grab him only to get knocked down by Steve's fist. The other two officers draw their guns, Steve blows them off and walks to Olivares who is sprinting to them yelling, "Easy! Guns down!"

Steve turns his back to them and rolls up his left sleeve revealing a tattoo on his inner forearm. The black tattoo depicts an ouroboros over a black square. Written on the snake's back, the message reads: *Mors vitae initium est.* He taps on it with one finger, it ripples like ink. He sticks his hand into the tattoo and pulls out a small cylindrical container. The container resembles a hollowed out pocket-watch; it's partially made from glass and brass. In it, flickers a yellow light resembling a firefly.

Olivares reaches Steve who's still got guns aimed at him. Olivares steps between the officers and Steve, "Guns down, damn it! Steve, what are you doing?"

"Finding whoever did this. When I do, I'll let you know," Steve starts running. His eyes are glued to the light in his hand. *Show me where.* The light floats and moves, pushing against a certain direction. *Lead me to it!*

Andrew enters the restroom of a gas station. He's panting against the wall. After catching his breath, he starts washing the blood and gasoline off him. The cold water relieves the pulsing heat trapped in his knuckles. He looks up at his reflection, he wipes two drops of blood off his face and smiles, "Thank you. I expected to wait for much longer. But you—you quench my thirst."

He nods as he looks ever so slightly over his shoulder. His eyes widen and he looks down, his smile evaporates as the door opens. Andrew leaves before the man that entered has the opportunity to interact. He walks into the gas station and heads straight to the fridges. With a blue sports drink in hand he heads to the cashier.

"Late night, huh?" the cashier says.

Andrew nods without uttering a word. He pays and leaves. He wanders the city of Chicago as he drinks, "Are you sure?

Sounds ... impossible. No, no, it isn't doubt. I'm sorry, please forgive—What? Where?" Andrew turns around and sees across the street a man in a trench coat running in his direction.

Andrew begins running and takes the first right turn. A nightclub a few buildings down is closing, releasing a horde of drunk and partied-out people. He mixes himself in with the crowd.

Steve sees the *guiding light* move vigorously as he gets closer to the target. It leads him to a crowd exiting a nightclub. *Too many people. Shit.* He looks at the crowd trying to see who doesn't belong. His eyes bounce from one person to the next. Steve gets closer to the crowd while keeping one eye on the light.

As he gets about two yards from the crowd, the light begins spinning like a compass entering the Bermuda Triangle. *What? A counter spell? It knows I'm looking for it.* He pockets his guiding light and begins to feel the weight of defeat. *Think Steve, do something!* He immediately pulls out his phone and begins recording the crowd. Everyone shows up, the video's focus and definition is clear. Everyone except one, *Found you!*

Steve speeds up, he starts weaving through the crowd using his phone as a kind of lookingglass.

"Hey!" someone yells. "Why you recording my girl?"

"What? I'm busy, get lost," Steve replies without looking at who is yelling at him. An explosive fist hits Steve across the face unexpectedly. The surrounding sounds of the crowd fade as his ears ring violently. The floor shifts from underneath Steve. He watches his phone fly out of his hand, shattering on the floor. As he lands on his face, a shockwave of pain barrels through him. He looks up, Steve sees a man around twenty-three or so waving his arm from pain.

"How you like that? You can't go around recording random people!" The man shouts at Steve. By this point, the crowd has turned around and is surrounding them.

He calmly gets back to his feet, picks up his ruined phone, and waves his hand across the air snapping his fingers. The snap creates a vibrant green spark. The crowd begins to disperse seconds later with blank stares as if under hypnosis. The man who hit him now has a thousand-yard stare as he too leaves abruptly in a zombie-like shuffle. He continues forward as he feels his jaw aching more and more. He checks his guiding light since his phone is destroyed, but it still spins recklessly. *Damn counter spell.* He looks around, there's no one left. *Great, you lost them, Steve.*

Steve leans on his knees and tries to disarm the vise clamped on his chest. His hands bite down on his knees like vicious pit bulls. He can feel his grasp on the situation slipping. His heartbeat speeds up, followed by a cold sweat. *No, snap out of it. You are in control!*

He distracts himself by taking his phone and snapping his fingers. The spiderweb-cracks on the screen disappear leaving the phone like new. He scrolls through his contacts and makes a call. The line rings once before it's answered, "Yeah, meet me at the diner by the precinct," he said. "I'll explain why I freaked out."

FEAR

Steve goes directly to the diner. He sees a patrol car parked. As he enters, Olivares sticks his hand up like an eager schoolboy. Steve sits down, he doesn't greet his childhood friend, instead he just says, "That last case—it will be impossible for you guys to solve. Whoever did it ... is like me."

The serious expression on Olivares' face slid right off, leaving him pale and wide-eyed. "So what now? I thought you said this kind of stuff couldn't happen."

"It's not supposed to. It has happened before but there are countermeasures for these situations—"

"So do you report it? How do *they* handle it?"

"Quiet down! People are staring. It's never good to see a cop freak out. Things aren't fully functional at the moment. Remember that I told you that there was a kind of coup/civil war between the two main factions I belong to?"

Olivares nods, but he still holds on to the same worried look.

"Okay, well ... the factions are restructuring themselves from the ground up. My kind—"

Olivares interrupts, "Wizards, right?"

"The term is *casters* but yes, basically. Look, I'm trying to tell you that I doubt they'll pay attention unless things get really out of control. I'll try to deal with it, but I need to let go of the other case. I can't afford any distractions."

"Yeah, whatever you need. Crap! How do I justify you dropping the case?" Olivares grabs his head as if it could fall off.

Steve replies while getting the attention of a nearby busboy, "I'll handle that." Steve turns to the busboy and asks him to get a server, he continues, "I need to refuel. In the meantime, tell me everything you have on the burnt-up guy."

"His name's Lawrence Hill, student, no criminal charges. Nothing about him is interesting. The guy was completely normal. We found his car not too far from the crime scene. Other than that, nothing. The autopsy hasn't been released yet. That's all."

"I'll have to talk to him. Can you get me into the morgue?" Olivares nods as Cece the waitress approaches. She takes their order and returns with their meal. They eat and chit-chat about trivial things, trying to decompress. Steve orders the check and tells Olivares, "My treat. I'm sorry for causing a scene back there. I could've han—"

"Handled it better? Yeah, but I don't blame you. What's with that dumb smirk on your face?"

Steve shows Olivares the bill, "Waitress gave me her number."

Olivares scoffs, "Let's go." They arrived at the morgue shortly after. Steve waits outside while Olivares speaks with the coroner. A short while later, Olivares comes out saying, "I got you fifteen minutes. Hurry up, and you owe me fifty bucks."

"Sure. I'll be right back," Steve says, closing the door. He locks it and draws the same symbol over the door as with Lucy's case. Wasting no time, he walks right to the autopsy table. On it rests the charred body of Lawrence Hill. *Damn, looks like he was crawling away as he died.* He hovers his hand over the body, he murmurs in complete silence and holds his breath, he snaps his fingers—waiting. Waiting for the veil to tear.

A wheezing gasp breaks the silence, "What happened? Why am I—"

"Hi, my name is Steve, can you tell me your name?"

Through ragged breathing and a raspy voice he replies, "Lawrence. Why did I return? I want to go back there. I need—"

"Yes, Lawrence, I know. I get that one a lot. We don't have much time, I need you to focus and answer a few questions. Afterwards, I promise you will return to *The Fountain*. Can you do that for me?"

Lawrence hesitates, groans, and says, "Alright."

"What's the last thing you remember? Please give me as many details as you can."

"A man gave me a ride. He attacked me and then I tasted gasoline."

"Did he give you a name?"

"Yes, after I introduced myself. I think. It could have been before. He said it was Andrew."

"Before he attacked you, did he do or say anything interesting, something that stuck out?"

"I, um, yes ... he—he mentioned St. Lawrence."

"What about him?"

"He asked if I knew the story."

"Do you remember what he looked like? Was he alone?"

"Bald, medium-ish build. He was sitting when it started and I couldn't see after that. He had a real gentle voice. A little too calm. He smiled too. We were alone."

Unsure of how much longer he could maintain Lawrence with the living, Steve asks, "Lawrence, would you mind if I had a *copy* of your last few moments alive?"

"How? I don't understand," his breathing starts to quicken. Steve knows time is almost up.

"Don't worry about how. Do I have your permission?"

"I—I guess."

Steve grabs Lawrence's calcined head, he feels the skin half-melted over the skull. He concentrates and feels his head pounding away. Bits of the attack flash over to Steve's mind. The pounding in his head escalates to a full-blown migraine. He stops, he hovers his hands over Lawrence again and turns his palms up. Lawrence exhales, returning to the afterlife.

Steve's knees buckle under his weight, he falls coughing. The white tiled floor turns red from the blood he spits out. *I know! I know! Stop, I gave him back already!* Steve takes a moment to recover, the symbol over the door is long gone. As he exits, he tells Olivares, "I got it. We need to discuss this but not now. Give me until tomorrow."

Olivares nods, knowing magic has a literal cost and if pushed enough, a deadly toll on the body. Olivares helps his friend get home.

Andrew looks at the calendar on the kitchen of the apartment he's rented. He was nearly caught two nights ago. He knows he's protected, yet something weighs him down. He takes the key on the counter and leaves. He drives around Chicago aimlessly, every once in a while he looks through his rear-view mirror; his eyes fixed on one of the back seats.

No one is there, yet he nods replying, "I know. Yes, I will grant you another sacrifice. Now? It's too soon. No! Wait, fine, fine. Now." Andrew parks his car, he walks around, and after a while ends up outside an empty church. "Here? Fine." He walks in, takes a seat, and absorbs the serene atmosphere. The service has just ended, he sees the altar boys leaving, and the priest gets ready too. He sees Andrew sitting in a pew at the back. Andrew stands up and walks over to him, he smiles politely making little eye contact. "Hello, could I keep you from going home for a few minutes?"

"Of course, son. How can I help?"

"I need to get something off my chest."

"Ah. You need a confession. This way," the priest leads Andrew to the confessional.

They sit down, a few mute seconds pass, "Bless me, Father, for I have sinned. My last confession was so long ago I can't remember it. I've always had dark thoughts. Awful thoughts. I never acted upon them until ... well, a few months ago. I—no, I can't tell you."

"Son, you've made it this far. You can tell me."

"No, no I can't. I'm not sure you or anyone can ever understand."

"What's your name? I'm father Samuel B. Young. I haven't seen you around here."

"I'm not from here. I think I better go." Andrew stands up and whispers, "He doesn't fit the agreed pattern. His name? Yes, yes." He sits back down, "I know it's none of my business but what's the B in your name stand for?"

Father Samuel smiles, "Bartholomew. It's not a common name now, but it was."

"Yes, I know. I'm well aware of St. Bartholomew's story," Andrew replies as he struggles to contain himself. His leg starts jittering but he immediately stops himself. He takes deep breaths and continues, "Perhaps I should confess."

"Of course, I'm here for you."

"I'm Andrew, you asked and I didn't reply. Sorry."

Father Samuel shakes his head waiting for Andrew to continue.

"Like I was saying, a few months back I—I felt like if I didn't fulfill my desire, I would go insane. So I did it. I finally did it after years."

"Did *what*, son?"

"I killed somebody. I—I needed to. Something spoke to me from inside."

Father Samuel stares at Andrew, the only thing separating them is the confessional screen. His silhouette removes most facial features but there's enough light for his smile to come through. "Apart from it being a crime, you know murder is a sin. A major one."

"I do, Father. I do. I felt terrible about it, at first. She was so young and pretty. You sound different. Am I making you nervous?"

"If I'm being honest ... yes, yes you are. I've never had such a confession before. Nonetheless, this is part of the job. Continue, please."

"I assumed that I would be satisfied. A one-time act. The darkness I had always heard in the back of my mind started getting stronger. I had it under control too. But then, I could *see* him. He's incredible, and he's made me understand so much. He explained to me that there's no such thing as absolute good or evil. And he's right."

Father Samuel stands up saying, "Andrew, you *see* someone who is justifying your actions? Actions that aren't acceptable. You need help. I can guide you to seek professional help." He's now standing directly across from Andrew.

Andrew stares politely, he sees Father Samuel sweating, and his hands are shaking. Andrew stands up and asks, "You think I'm crazy, don't you?" He shakes his head, "Don't worry, Father, I know I'm not. The second kill was easier, much more satisfying too. I can't stop. I don't want to. He protects me. I give you my word, Father ... you'll do your name justice." Andrew unfolds the knife he's had in his pocket all day.

Father Samuel starts to run. Andrew follows, catching up quickly. He slams the hilt on the back of Father Samuel's head. The dry crack of skull on steel makes Andrew smile. He stands over the dazed priest, his head bleeds, and some of it gets on a pew. Andrew mounts him, he carefully cuts off the cassock so he doesn't damage his prey. It takes him a short while.

Father Samuel tries to move but his efforts are doused by Andrew as he bashes his head on the floor. Blood pools after a rather loud crack, Andrew checks his handy work by pulling Father Samuel's head back. It's a fractured nose. Father Samuel pants and groans with a twisted and distorted face, all while Andrew's expression is like that of a child opening birthday presents.

Andrew runs the side of his knife along father Samuel's cheek and says, "I'll be quick, promise." And without missing the pace, Andrew plunges his knife into Father Samuel's back.

Steve looks at the clock on his kitchen wall. It's 9:00 in the morning. *In five, four, three, two ...*

DING—DONG. "I brought bagels." Olivares' voice breaks through the door after the doorbell rings.

Steve opens the door for Olivares, the two nod at each other. "We have a lot to talk about. So you wanna eat before or after?"

"How messed up is it?"

"From my POV, about a seven or eight."

"POV?" Olivares tilts his head with his question.

"You know what? Screw it, I'm starving. We talk over breakfast." They sit down, Olivares places the bag of bagels on the kitchen table as Steve pours coffee. On the table rests a plate of lox, spreadable cream cheese, fresh berries, and mini muffins.

"What did you find out, Steve?"

With his mouth full of bagel, Steve mumbles, "I think there are cases that involve the same killer. In fact, I wonder if Lucy was one of them. I'm not certain yet. I'll need access to past cases. Think you could get me access?"

"I think so. Why do you think there are more cases?" Olivares replies while spreading cream cheese on his bagel.

Steve shakes his head, he grabs it and presses on his temples, "The victim, he told me that the killer mentioned St. Lawrence. He was burnt alive, just like the victim. They have the same name. I didn't think anything of it until I remembered the case before this one."

"The one at the hotel?"

Steve nods, he takes two blueberries and places them on an empty plate. He points to them, "The victim had her eyes plucked out on display. That's important. It has to mean something. Her name was Lucy, just like St. Lucy who was beheaded after her eyes were removed. Could be a coincidence, but you know how rare coincidences are in our line of work."

Olivares stops chewing, he nods over and over, "Now I have to get you to look at unsolved cases."

"I also took a look at how Lawrence died."

Olivares stares at Steve and squints. He opens his mouth as if wanting to speak but soon stops himself. He takes a moment and says, "I don't—how?"

"You really want to know or are you just confused?"

"Confused," Olivares admits.

"I saw his face. Clear as day too. I'm not sure why, but he seems so familiar. I just don't remember from where."

"Can't you do something to *make* you remember?"

Steve shakes his head, "Magic doesn't work like that. Not this time. It's not as simple as snapping your fingers. Some spells require much more, while others only need a simple snap. Since I saw him in someone else's memory, my mind forgets details fast. Any spell I try will only waste time. Let's finish eating so you can take me to see those files."

Olivares nods. They eat and about an hour later they head over to the precinct. Steve doesn't say a word as they head straight to the file room, along the way, he stumbles into the officer he assaulted. Steve nods politely, the officer turns to Olivares demanding, "What's he doing here?"

"Easy. He's with me. He thinks he has something on the Hill case."

The officer gets right in Steve's face, he's so close Steve can feel the officer breathing on him.

Steve asks, "Ever heard of personal space? No? Shame, you should try it." Steve slips out of the officer's way and continues on his way.

Just before he's out of earshot he hears, "Keep messing with cops like that, and you won't live to tell the tale."

Steve ignores him. Olivares and Steve arrive at the file room. They sign in, and as soon as they're inside, Steve shuts and jams the door.

"What are you doing?"

"Sorry, but I need to search *my* way. Besides, I don't want any interruptions. I'm not going through hours of footage and tons of reports, one at a time. Sit down, I'll only take a—"

PING! Steve's phone chimes notifying him of a new text message. He takes a look and smiles. He opens the text and reads: *Hi Steve, I'm good, thank you for asking. No, I'm free next weekend. See you then.*

Steve texts back: *Great, see you then.* "Like I was saying, I'll only take a second."

"Is that who I think it is?" Olivares asks. "You're smiling and you rarely smile."

"Shut up."

"Oh no. Only two things make you smile like that. One of them is cats. and cats don't text. The other one was my sister ... Wait—the waitress makes you smile!"

"*Cece*, her name is Cece," Steve corrects Olivares. "Let me work. Also, be quiet. I need silence for this spell." Steve closes his eyes, erases the smile on his face, and extends his arms out. His breathing deepens, it becomes controlled, conscious. He turns his left palm up, leaving his right facing down. Clearing his throat, he says carefully, "Visa mig vilddjuret gömt i klar syn, o kunskapens herre. Visa det för mig, Mimir." The lights flicker, and Steve begins to feel the expected tingling through his hands.

"Did it work?"

"Shh! It will. These things aren't always instantaneous, sometimes they—" Steve's eyes roll back leaving them white. His right hand lowers as his left points forward. Steve groans, he begins walking or rather stumbling around as if his body is being piloted by someone else. He skims through a file cabinet and pulls out a folder. He continues and walks over to the computer and begins pulling footage from a security camera. Through tense and warped lips Steve says, "Här ligger bestarna du soker." Steve coughs, returning to normal. He covers his mouth and tastes blood.

"You alright man? I—I don't know what you said," Olivares explains walking over to Steve.

"I'm fine. Give me a minute," Steve replies, catching his breath. His heart bashes mercilessly on his chest, neck, gums, and even eyes. "Thank you, Mimir," Steve says faintly.

"Who's Mimir? And what did you say? I know it's not English."

"A Norse god. I told him, 'Show me the beast hidden in plain sight, O lord of knowledge. Show it to me, Mimir.' Afterwards, I heard him reply, 'Here lie the beasts you seek.' Now please, tell me what happened. What did I do?"

"You grabbed a case file and pulled the footage from a security camera. It looks like it's from the—Oh, okay, I think I'm catching on. This is footage from the Lucy Ricci case. And it looks like the file is Lucy's case file. So what now?"

Steve sits up and starts scrubbing through the footage. He doesn't reply.

BANG, BANG, BANG! Someone bangs on the door and yells, "You get out of there this instant, Norton!"

"Open it Olivares. I don't want to get you in more trouble."

Olivares does as Steve says. As soon as the door unlocks, it's kicked open by Detective Roberts. He pushes Olivares aside and marches directly to Steve. Roberts picks Steve up by his shirt as he yells, "You think you can come back here as if nothing happened?"

"I have work to do."

"You assaulted an officer and resisted arrest! You have balls, I'll give you that. You're under arrest." Detective Roberts begins handcuffing Steve, pinning him against the wall.

"Sir, please. You have to hear him out," Olivares tries explaining.

"I don't want to hear it, Olivares! You're lucky I haven't arrested you for not stopping him," Detective Roberts retorts.

"Steve has something on the case," Olivares says as he steps between Detective Roberts and the door.

"Like hell, he does."

"I do, actually. They're connected. The Ricci and Hill cases."

Detective Roberts turns Steve around, he pulls him close and warns him, "If you're messing with me, you won't see the outside world in years," he sits Steve down. "Now, elaborate."

Steve sits back and gets comfortable, "First off … I'd give my right eye to catch the killer. As for the cases, the culprit behind the Lawrence Hill case is most likely the same for the Lucy Ricci case. Both victims share names with catholic saints. They were killed like them too. Still think I'm lying?" Steve removes his handcuffs and offers them gum.

"How did you—" Roberts half asks, ignoring the gum.

"Take the cuffs off? Not important. We need to find the person responsible for this. People who share names with any saint are in serious danger. The city should know."

Detective Roberts nods. He walks around and asks Steve, "What names should we be looking out for?"

"Lucy and Lawrence are taken. We still have a lot but something tells me it's not just saints but the ones with the worst deaths. He likes to make his victims suffer. Off the top of my head, there's still Stephen, he was stoned, Sebastian was clubbed, Valentine was clubbed and stoned but there's hardly anyone left by that name. There's also Edmund, he was arrowed, Perpetua and Felicity were killed by slicing their necks but I think we can rule out Perpetua and focus on Felicity. Cecilia, she was badly beheaded … oh shit! Hold on." Steve pulls his phone out and calls Cece. He hears the line ringing, "Pick up. Please!"

Cece walks over to a table with a single person in it, he's reading the menu. She waves getting his attention and says, "Hello, I'll be your server today. My name is Cecilia, what can I get for you?"

The menu lowers and a bald man with a gentle smile replies, "Hi Cecilia, that's a nice name. I saw you here a few days ago. I was by the jukebox. I'm Andrew, a pleasure."

"Thank you. Likewise."

"I'll have two eggs, over-easy please, bacon and hash—"

RING, RING! "I'm sorry sir, I'll send it to voicemail," Cece explains.

"No, no. Please answer, it could be important."

"Really?"

"Yes."

Cece takes a look and sees Steve is calling, "Hi handsome, how are you?" Cece says as she answers her phone. "Um, okay. Weird but I trust you, Steve. Okay, bye." She turns her attention back to Andrew and says, "Sorry, so you want two eggs over-easy with a side of bacon and ... ?"

"Hash browns. Wheat toast please."

Cece nods and says, "Coming right up." She takes the menu, places the order, and goes to the break room to follow Steve's instructions.

Andrew's smile widens as he sees her leave. He nods at the reflection on the sugar dispenser in agreement.

Hearing her voice brings a smile back to Steve's face. "Hi, Cece, um, I just want you to do me a favor and please don't ask questions. I promise I'll explain later. It's very important that you remove your name tag from your uniform. Oh, and use an alias, please. Don't let anyone know your real name. Thanks, I'll see you later." Steve hangs up and returns to the officers, "Sorry, there's also Bartholomew he was skinned alive—"

"Woah, woah. Hold on," Roberts interrupts, pulling out his radio. *KSST!* "This is Detective Roberts, who's working on the priest murder case?" *KSST!*

A few seconds later he gets a reply, *KSST!* "Hey chief, Tomas is working it. Why?"

"What's the priest's name?"

"Samuel Young, sir."

"Is that his full name?"

"No, it's Samuel Bartholomew Young."

Detective Roberts and Steve turn to each other. Olivares blurts out, "Let's go people!"

The three get to Detective Roberts' car and head to the crime scene. Roberts lets them through, and that's when they see it. The body of Father Samuel Bartholomew Young stands in front of the altar, his skinless body posed as if in mid-prayer. His skin wraps him like a tunic.

"Shit!" Olivares says loudly, making everyone there lay eyes on him.

Detective Roberts turns to him and asks, "Would you like to repeat that a little louder? I don't think all of Chicago heard you."

"Sorry sir," Olivares replies.

Steve lets them get ahead, he walks slowly as he takes in Andrew's latest work. He tries to see a pattern he might have missed with the other two. *The victim seems to be praying but why?* He continues watching from afar for a few minutes but finds nothing. He joins the other two and asks, "So what's the story?"

"He was found earlier today by the security guard across the street. Apparently, they're friends. No one saw anything. Everything is just like the last two. No prints, hair, nothing," Roberts explains while deflating.

Steve nods, stretches, and says, "Will I be able to chat with him anytime soon?"

"You keep saying *chat* but they're dead. What do you actually do differently from us?"

"Nothing really, it's a figure of speech," Steve replies. "So? Can I?"

"Sure, give me a minute," Roberts says, leaving Steve and getting everyone out.

Olivares turns to Steve saying, "I'll leave you to it."

He waits for everyone to leave, once alone he starts a new piece of cinnamon gum and draws the theta nigrum over every entrance. He stands next to the body and hovers his hands over it. He murmurs and holds his breath before snapping his fingers.

"Why—why did you bring me back?"

"It'll be a quick chat, Father Samuel. I need to ask you about—"

"I know why you're here. You want to know more about Andrew. I've learned more than I would have imagined from

The Fountain. Time doesn't flow there like it does here on Earth. I know what you are, and I hope you know what you're getting into. I assumed someone like you would understand how cruel it is to bring someone back."

Steve stares at Father Samuel. "That's a first. What am I getting into exactly?"

"To you, I died last night. To me, I've just been born. I'm whole."

"We're wasting time. Tell me about him. Anything."

"He's not what you expect. You're special but he's *guided*. He seems normal, at first. Just before he attacked me—something shifted in him. Something different. By the time I noticed, it was too late. A dark power holds him. Send me back, please."

Steve can hear Father Samuel's voice wrapped in fatigue. Steve's head throbs, letting him know he's used this spell too many times this week. The unmistakable taste of iron travels across his tongue, he checks with his finger. The tip is a deep red. He sighs and says, "How's this, Father? I take the memory of your death and let you go. Agreed?"

"Yes, I want to return."

"I won't take long," Steve reaches out and grabs his head. His fingers feel the exposed muscles still somewhat moist. Steve groans and his face twists as he struggles to concentrate. The taste of blood grows stronger; the flavor and smell take his mind hostage. He spits in his hand and finally finds Father Samuel's last moments alive. A surge of pain strikes him from behind and he sees something odd. An *interloper*.

His knees buckle and he falls to his face. The steps to the altar catch him by the nose. *CRACK!* He hears something break far away. He can see the main entrance open, it's Olivares. Tunnel vision sets in. Olivares' voice echoes as everything turns black.

Andrew looks at his watch and sees it's almost 11 a.m. He watches the diner from across the street. His eyes never leave Cece. Half an hour later, Cece's shift ends. He stays locked on her and sees her walk out and head over to the bus stop. Andrew follows discreetly.

As the bus arrives, Andrew lets her and the other three people at the bus stop board, he waits for the last possible minute and boards. Andrew sits as far away from Cece as possible and keeps to himself. He keeps close attention to where she is.

After a while, Cece tugs on the stop-chord. The bus slows down to let passengers off. *HISS!* The air brakes release the pressurized air within making the bus come to a smooth stop. Cece and two people, including Andrew, get off. He checks his phone to put distance between Cece and himself. He follows her into an apartment complex and lets her get inside. The lock rattles after the door shuts.

Andrew waits fifteen minutes before knocking twice. A few seconds pass, and he raises his hand ready to knock again when the lock rattles unlocking the door. Cece cracks it open asking, "Yes? Can I help you?"

"Yes, thank you. I think I'm lost. Do you happen to know what apartment number Cecilia lives in?"

"I'm sorry but I don't know anyone by that name. Good luck." Cece begins closing the door only for it to hit something. She looks down and sees it's Andrew's foot.

"Aren't you the waitress that served me breakfast this morning? Cecilia, right?" Andrew says smiling with both mouth and eyes.

A gentle head shake is followed by her replying, "No, sorry you must have me mistaken for someone else. Have a good day."

His façade of a serene glee crumbles as he bursts through the door knocking Cece down. He quickly shuts the door, locking it. An improvised kick to the face barely makes contact with her face, only leaving a burning sensation across her jaw. She starts crawling away, but Andrew mounts her and grabs her as a muffled yell fails to escape from his unbreakable grip. His free hand wraps around the back of her head and bashes it face-first on the wood floor.

One bash is enough to daze her. He pulls her head up by her hair and whispers, "I hate when people lie. Tell me, Cecilia. Do you know the story of St Cecilia?"

Cece's crying all over Andrew's hand, she's shaking uncontrollably.

"Well? Answer me." Andrew says with the same calm from before.

Cece shakes her head, answering Andrew's question.

"Too bad. When I'm done with you ... your boyfriend Steve will always remember her tale."

Hearing Steve's name breaks Cece out of her fear-induced paralysis. She reaches for her phone and kicks frantically. Andrew immediately douses her fiery temper with a punch to the liver. Andrew feels her body get limp, he tosses her phone aside and with his belt ties her up. He then takes her socks and stuffs her mouth rendering her mute.

"Yes, I know I have to purposefully botch the job," Andrew says to the large mirror in the living room. He continues, "I'll see what she has available in the kitchen. I forgot to bring a dull knife. Please make sure she doesn't escape." Andrew takes several knives out and asks from the kitchen, "What knife? I don't know what that means. What's it look like? Yes, I see it."

Andrew returns to the living room and presents the mirror with a cleaver. He turns to Cece and kneels next to her. He gently brushes Cece's copper-brown hair off her sweaty face and says, "It'll be over soon Cecilia." She begins moving, attempting to free herself. Andrew raises the cleaver ready to swing down. He stops and says, "She'll bleed out before I finish."

Andrew turns back to the mirror, nodding repeatedly. His eyes and mouth widen, leaving him looking like a child who just came downstairs to see what Santa brought. The mirror begins rippling like a pool of mercury. A warped and distorted bell tolls from within it.

A hand covered in dried-up blood breaks the surface of the mirror, it stretches out grabbing the frame. The second hand does the same. A face surfaces, the bleached-gray skin accentuates his features, it contrasts with the elaborate scarification of his skin, still raw and bloody. His eyes are black storms with yellow irises. The humanoid smiles at Andrew, his teeth riddled with sharp hooked symbols carved directly on them.

He pulls himself out revealing himself entirely to both Andrew and Cece. Both are frozen in awe. Cece's face holds no expression; Andrew on the other hand is bowing to the being responsible for bringing his biggest urges and desires to fruition. The being is topless and wears a long dark gray skirt down to his feet. A distorted Metatron's cube is carved on his chest using negative space for its lines. Reaching to his back, he rips out two metal hooks from his skin.

Holding them with open hands he shuts his dark eyes opening his mouth. The hooks float to the ceiling as the distorted bell tolls again. Cece begins floating too, she hangs upright from nothing at all. Her screams get stuck in her throat as if they fear meeting the creature. The being turns to Andrew reaching to him, "Rise, summoner. You will be guided by my hands." The being's voice scratches at listeners from within the ears. A hallucinatory voice.

Andrew follows orders. Upon getting up, the being stands behind Andrew and touches Andrew's wrists with his. He begins swinging away empty-handed. Andrew's body starts swinging away with him. Andrew's expression shifts from that child-like wonder to a confused surprise.

"Fear not summoner. I'll pull the strings this time," the being explains. Andrew watches as he is now literally a living puppet on invisible strings. His body mimic's the movement of the being. Every swing lands heavily on Cece's neck and despite the blade's sharp nature, her neck resists it. Each swing paints the pale yellow walls of her living room with rich currant spatter.

Cece's eyes are forced open by some invisible force. Her neck slowly splits open, pain strikes lightning fast. Both her and Andrew hear the wet whacking of the cleaver accompanied by her gurgling throat. "She's choking! Do something! She won't last!" Andrew pleads.

The being replies between swings, "No—" *WHACK!* "she'll be—" *WHACK!* "fine. She feels it all." *WHACK!* "The pain, the—" *WHACK!* "blood loss," *WHACK!* "the urge to—" *WHACK!* "breathe. Overstimulation via—" *WHACK!* "exquisite pain."

And with a last swing, Andrew sees what he wanted most, a near-perfect replica of the botched beheading of St Cecilia. Her head hanging from a deceitfully strong strand of skin. Permanently frozen on her face are her bulging eyes, and clamped jaw.

The invisible strings sever, freeing Andrew. "Pose her," the being orders. Andrew gets to work. After a short while, he asks, "Can I follow the plan we discussed?"

"Of course, summoner."

———ele———

Ammonia with a hint of lavender shakes Steve back to life. "Easy Steve, you fainted," Olivares tells him.

Steve tries sitting up, only for vertigo to topple him down. He looks around and sees he's still at the crime scene. "How long was I out?" Steve asks.

"About an hour. One of the medics took a look at you. Told us not to move you. He said you're fine, but I got worried. I used my smelling salts. You broke your nose on the way down."

Steve makes sure no one else can hear them. He pulls Olivares in and whispers, "I saw something. The priest—he showed me some ... *thing*. I—I have to stop him." Steve barely manages to get up, "I have to go. I—"

Olivares grabs Steve, telling him, "Stop it! Look at yourself. You can barely walk."

"I'm fine. I'll text you when I—"

SLAP! Olivares interrupts Steve with a good slap. "Go home. You need to rest. Your *skills* have a steep price. You've worked too hard this week. I'll see you tomorrow morning at your place. It's my day off."

Steve nods, knowing his friend is right. He ignores the crackling embers Olivares spread across his face, "See you tomorrow then. Good slap, strong."

Olivares forces a smile. He waves goodbye and before Steve leaves, says, "Oh your phone got a few texts while you were out. It's Cece. Go see her. Be vulnerable with her. Women love that from time to time. It'll help you relax. It's been almost ten years since Diana's death. It's time."

"Yeah, I will." Steve leaves the church, calls himself a ride, and checks his phone.

Six texts from Cece. Let's see.

Hey handsome. I don't want to wait till next week to see you. - an hour ago

Steve, come on. I promise I'll make it worthwhile. - 50 minutes ago

I know you're busy, text me when you're free. - 45 minutes ago

Okay, I'll try to sweeten the deal. We order pizza, watch a movie and see what happens. Deal? - 13 minutes ago

Still nothing? You're hard to convince. Okay, final offer. I'll wear this the whole time and nothing else. - 25 minutes ago

Attached to the text is her address and a picture of a pair of black lace panties placed on the edge of her bed.

Steve smiles and chuckles, he lets her know he's coming and gets into his ride. He gives the driver the address to Cece's place. On the way there, something crosses his mind. *This doesn't sound like Cece. Well, it's not like I know her that well. Guess she really likes me. No, this—* Steve shakes his head. *No Steve, get out of your head. Enjoy it.*

Steve arrives at the apartment building and heads straight to Cece's place. He stands directly at the door waiting. *Calm down, take your time, and breathe.* Steve knocks and the door gives way. Without entering, Steve asks, "Cece? Are you home?" The lack of a response isn't something Steve's used to. He enters the apartment and says loudly, "I'm sorry I didn't reply earlier. Before you come out here in your little attire, I should warn you, I'm in no shape for—"

Steve's eyes freeze along with the rest of him. At the end of the living room by the corner, there she is. Cece's corpse sitting on a kitchen chair holding her head on her lap. A slim strand of skin still uniting body and head. Steve tries to speak, to say something, anything, but no word leaves his mouth. He breaks free from the shock and runs to her. He reaches for her but holds back knowing there's nothing to do.

"No, please. Not again. Not again!" He drops to his knees and pounds his fists on the floor. "Cece, I'm sorry! I—I should have protected you!" Steve bellows out of impotence.

"You can't stop me, Steve."

The sudden break of silence forces Steve to turn to the direction of the noise. From inside the mirror he sees Andrew wave as he walks away. "Come back. Face me!" Steve shouts. He heads to the mirror ready to chase after Andrew. He stops, turns back to Cece's body one last time, and returns his attention to the mirror.

Steve extends his hands out and unites his thumbs with palms out. A pair of smoky shadow-arms extend out from his own and travel down and through the mirror. He manages to grab onto something and begins pulling. A second later, he's pulled with an inhuman force. Steve is slammed against the mirror so hard that his face slips inside it.

Inside it, he sees the creature pull him in. He smiles at him and says, "You are no ordinary caster. I haven't seen an *umbramancer* in centuries. Manipulation of shadows is a rare and difficult skill."

"I saw you with the priest. You're the thing protecting this—this freak! Why?"

"Watch your tongue, caster. I am no *thing*. You should know what I am, given your branch of magic. In comparison to you, I am more alive than all of humanity combined. I need no reason to protect my summoner. I grow tired of this conversation." The creature rips the shadows holding on to him and walks away, escorting Andrew.

"Wait!" Steve shouts, chasing them through the mirrored realm. The creature raises a red hand warping the mirrored realm they traverse. Each step Steve takes sends him back miles. By the time Steve finds his way out and back into Cece's apartment, it is now late at night. The kitchen clock says 3 a.m.

Wasting no time, Steve plunges his hand inside his portal tattoo pulling out a selenite sphere and whispers into it. He stares at Cece's corpse and shakes his head, already dreading his decision. *Please work.* Steve's heart skips a necessary beat as he tries for a Hail Mary, he slams the selenite orb as hard as humanly possible against the ground, shattering it. Now he can only wait. One second, two, then three pass in a sobering silence. The guilt and weight of Cece's death begins to strangle Steve, then thunder strikes back.

Very well caster, you have my attention. We'll see you then.

The creature's reply infiltrates Steve's thoughts. The reply is so deafeningly loud that it takes him a full minute to recover. Once ready, Steve leaves the apartment and heads out into the pouring rain. Steve taps on his portal tattoo and pulls out his *sand transporter,* a hollowed out pocket watch filled with golden sand. He pictures *The Bean*, located in Millennium Park and presses the only button on the device.

Gravity shifts from under him, its pull sends him forward. Just before he flies off, his body disintegrates into sand for the wind to take. A couple of seconds pass until his feet slam to the ground, his stomach protests as he's still not fully reformed. Once complete, Steve stands across from Cloud Gate—The Bean.

Given the time and weather, Millenium Park is nearly empty. From inside the mirror-finished sculpture, the creature walks out. "It's the first time I've been contacted through an *angel's whisper*, I enjoyed the pain it brought. Your promise of pain and madness is the only reason we agreed to meet you. Do not waste our time," the creature says.

Steve walks over to them, he takes a second to organize his thoughts, "You said there's no agreement between you two. I—"

"Oh we've reached an agreement," the creature interrupts. "I have no reason as to why I protect him."

Steve nods, "Right, I just don't understand one thing." Steve snaps his fingers causing the rain to go around him as if holding an invisible umbrella.

"Speak, caster!"

"Why is a demon as powerful as yourself, volunteering as a familiar to an ordinary human like him? It's beneath you, isn't it? Why not choose a caster?"

Steve's words force Andrew out from underneath the Bean, "Someone like you? Please!" Andrew turns to the creature saying, "Pay no attention to him, he's scared shitless. He knows he can't stop me. Let's go Azm—"

"Speak my name and you'll beg for death!" the creature warns Andrew with a dismissive shove. "Don't attempt to understand, caster. Now give me what I came for, or I'll take it from you."

"Look, I'm not going to fight you. That's suicidal. Instead, I propose that you leave him, allowing me to deliver him to the authorities. In exchange, you join me in taking out other freaks like him. Outside the law, that is. Pain and madness guaranteed," Steve explains while keeping a firm eye on Andrew.

The creature turns to Andrew and back to Steve. He asks, "It's a tempting offer, yet I seek instant gratification."

Steve nods and sighs. He points at his right eye, "Make the deal with me, and I'll rip my eye out. Final offer."

A lustful smile stretches over the creature's face. His blood-covered teeth resemble the red smiles of clowns. "Now that's an offer," he turns to Andrew and asks, "Care to counter it?"

Andrew hesitates, "You're joking, right? I've killed for you!"

"Wrong! You've killed for yourself. I've been protecting you while watching. I've been enjoying the spectacle." The creature grabs Andrew by the face and says, "I can taste your fear. Your lack of a spine disappoints me."

Steve asks, "Is that a yes?"

"Hold on!" Andrew buts in, "We make a great team. Besides, I've shown you what the media calls me. You want to stop now that we have the whole city trembling?"

Steve asks, "What are you talking about?"

"The Saint Maker. That's what they call me on the news. After the priest was found, the police warned all citizens with the names of saints," Andrew replies proudly. He turns to the creature, "We continue this indefinitely. That's my counteroffer."

"More of the same isn't much of a counter," Steve comments.

"Shut up! I'm not talking to you!" Andrew shouts.

"The umbramancer is right. A boring offer," the creature walks over to Steve and whispers, "Actions speak louder than words." He then licks Steve across the face and offers to shake hands.

Steve inhales sharply, "Make sure he doesn't run away." Both shake hands, sealing the deal. Steve pulls out a small pocket knife and immediately shoves it between his eye and skull. The shrill screams from his nerve endings ripping apart and the agony in himself takes him to his knees. The creature moans and licks his lips as he watches Steve blind himself.

With trembling hands and breathing heavily, Steve feels his eye collapse within the socket. Clumsily he gropes at his face and pulls it out. Barely conscious and drenched in sweat, rain, and blood, Steve holds his hand out for the creature to see.

The sound of applause from above followed by his twisted voice reaches Steve's ears, "Bravo, caster. I've seen many men fail to maim others let alone themselves." Taking the offering, the creature turns around. He tastes the severed eye and tells Andrew, "Our little adventure was fun. We'll meet again."

Andrew is unable to move. He pleads, "I'll give you my soul! It's much better than an eye, isn't it?"

Chuckling, the creature replies, "A myth. What would a demon do with a soul? More importantly, a demon never goes back on a sealed deal. A demon's word is ironclad. Since I can still read your mind, yes, I'm not letting you move. Now sleep."

Andrew falls into a deep sleep. Steve manages to get up and calls the authorities.

A few days later, Steve is escorted by his friend, Officer Olivares, to an interrogation room. "He's already told us everything, you don't have to do this. Are you sure you should be alone with that creep? He took your eye," Olivares says.

"I want to show him something. I'll be fine," Steve replies as he turns the door knob. Before entering, he says, "Oh, do me one favor. Turn off the camera and don't look."

Olivares nods.

"Why are you here?" Andrew asks.

"Pain and madness. That's what I promised him. I had to sever seven muscles to remove my eye! The pain was excruciating, but I'm still sane," Steve shouts and grabs Andrew's head forcing him to face the two-way mirror. He explains, "I'll tell you a secret about demons and other interdimensional beings. They take a temporary form for our mind to understand. It's for our safety. Witness his true form!"

Steve shuts his eye and peels back Andrew's eyelids, forcing him to see the mirror. Andrew's frantic screams flood the interrogation room. Steve feels Andrew struggling against the metal table he's cuffed to. "This is for all the people you killed, especially Cece. Rot in hell, piece of shit!" Steve exits the room covering his eye. With the door safely closed, he opens his eye and stops Olivares from entering by blocking the way.

"What did you do to him?"

Steve tells him, "All I did was show him what true madness is." He turns back to the door, snaps his fingers at the door and exhales, releasing the tension trapped in his chest, "Now it's safe."

PATIENT #41

by Jose Francisco Trevino Chavez

*C*LICK. The sound of the record button being pressed breaks the silence in the room. The cassette tape starts spinning. "This is Dr. Edwards recording patient log number two. Date is November twentieth of 1998. Patient's name is Walter Thomas, patient number forty-one, currently undiagnosed. The patient and myself have only met once prior to this session. That was session zero. This is session one. Walter, hello. How are you feeling today? Your file says you aren't sleeping well. Why don't you tell me what's going on?"

A wide pair of brown eyes jump from one place to the next. *It's just the doctor and me. We're alone.* Walter clears his throat and says, "You know, you've read the file."

Dr. Edwards sighs as he rubs his temples. He takes the patient file next to him, opens it, and reads aloud, "Despite rigorous testing, Walter Thomas shows no sign of schizophrenia, early onset dementia, or any other mental illness that can explain what he claims." He closes the file and gently places it back where it was a moment ago. From behind thick glasses, a half-opened pair of blue eyes meet Walter's. He says, "Walter, there's nothing wrong with you. I don't want to be rude, but I have to ask, are you doing this for attention?"

"How dare you? You yourself recognized that I suffered from anxiety attacks shortly after I was sent here. I'm not faking!" Walter's eyes flood over and his breath shallows. He takes a second to compose himself. *One, two, three, four, five.* He continues, "I'm scared doc. *He'll* visit tonight. He does so once a week."

"Walter, you are in a psychiatric hospital where each patient has their own room. The rooms are locked electronically and the windows don't open. No one is going to visit you. It's impossible."

Walter ejects himself from his seat, sending the chair flying back. *CRASH!* "Like hell it is!" Jumping forward, Walter takes Dr. Edwards by his tie, pulling him in close. "Why won't anybody take me seriously?"

Dr. Edwards shouts, "I need some help!"

The door immediately opens up and a large man in green scrubs enters. He pulls Walter back like a ragdoll. The man slams Walter against the wall and turns to Dr. Edwards, who says, "Don't hurt him. I'm fine, thanks. We're done for today. Before you take him to his room, I want to tell him something." Dr. Edwards walks up to Walter and says, "No one is coming for you."

Walter wants to say something, but he's still recovering from the nurse's bear strength, so instead he just waits for them to drag him back to his room. Back in his room, the nurse tells him, "I'm not here to hurt you, I don't want to do that. There are a lot of dangerous patients here. I'm sorry for slamming you. Are we good?"

Walter stares at him but doesn't reply. He just nods.

Several hours and a stomach full of rotisserie chicken later, Walter sits on his bed. *Nine o'clock. Light's out is an hour away, think. There has to be a way to show them.* He sits there brainstorming. After several failed ideas, Walter looks at the clock on his nightstand again. *Shit! Two minutes left.* Walter changes into his pajamas and brushes his teeth.

He stands across his bed. His palms sweat. His heart pounds almost threatening to burst out of his chest. With a deep breath, he slides under the covers. A second later his room is devoured by darkness. Walter immediately shields himself with his sheets. The piercing sound of silence is all Walter hears. Minutes slither away like a traveling slug. *Sleep Walt, maybe he won't come.* His mind grasps at smoke-like hope. Walter squeezes his eyes shut and waits for Morpheus. The heavy veil of dreams wraps itself around him, far off in the depths of his mind, he feels his body sinking.

A pleasant, gentle force, like a weighted blanket, he can feel its soft touch. The blanket stiffens and shifts, ultimately sliding off him. The force, however, gets heavier and solidifies over him. Something crawls across Walter's chest. The long spider-like crawl captures his attention, and his heart races again. Still from within the safety of his slumber, Walter thinks, *No, no, no! It's here. On me. Wake up! WAKE UP!*

"There, there. No need to struggle, you won't move." Its raspy voice lets Walter know. "Tonight you will not give." A gasoline-drenched razor of a laugh forces Walter to open his eyes. In an ocean of darkness, a pair of glowing garnets lock onto Walter's eyes. Unable to move, like a fleshy sculpture, he feels the spidery crawl of long fingers pry his mouth open and deposit a fig-sized object down his throat. "Rejoice Walter! You've been chosen. We will meet again in a week. Now rest." As the creature's voice infiltrates Walter's ears, he loses consciousness.

―•❦•―

CLICK. The tape recorder starts again. "This is Dr. Edwards recording patient log number three. The date is November twenty-seven of 1998. Patient's name is Walter Rogers, he's patient number forty-one. Currently, he is still undiagnosed. Hello, Walter, how are you feeling today?" Dr. Edwards is only met by Walter's silence. "My notes say that you've been forced to eat something. Why don't you tell me what happened?"

"Will you take me seriously this time?" Walter's voice held equal parts resentment and helplessness. Dr. Edwards nods. Walter continues, "That thing paid me a visit that night—the night you said he couldn't possibly get in."

"The one tormenting you?" Dr. Edwards asks, dropping his hands to his lap as they ball up into fists.

"Yes! Aren't you listening?" Walter shouts. "It actually touched me this time. I—I can't move when it's around." His brown eyes lower to his hands. A tear escapes from one eye. It crashes on the table creating a small and delicate mirror. Walter catches his minuscule self staring back, he hunches down and says, "Something about its dark red eyes, maybe it's that demonic screeching it calls a voice. Either way, it takes control and ... I can't move after that."

Dr. Edwards stares at Walter, studies his body language. *That kind of fear can't be faked. He really believes something is visiting him,* he writes down on his notes. "What does it want from you, Walter?"

Shaking his head, Walter shrugs in defeat. "I don't know. It said I was *chosen*. But it didn't say what for."

"Did it say anything else?" Dr. Edwards asks as he takes several notes on what Walter is saying.

"No, just that it's returning tonight. Please, doctor, I need help," Walter pleads.

Dr. Edwards nods, and after thinking it over, he says, "Alright, I'll help you if you help me. How's that sound?"

Walter glares at him, then nods. "Great. I'll get a guard to stay right outside your room. You will take a small dose of an antipsychotic. Agreed?" He asks as he extends his hand.

Walter shakes the doctor's hand. "Fine, but the damn pill won't work."

"I'll see you next week Walter. Things will change from this point on, you'll see."

Later that night, Walter stands across from his bed. The clock on his nightstand is a minute away from nine. He stares at it, he breathes in and ... the lights shut off. Walter stiffens up, each muscle frozen solid. As he exhales, he feels the cold air leaving his mouth. A light smile sneaks onto Walter's face. *It's not cold, it's your toothpaste idiot.* He lets out a chuckle and tells himself, *Just get in bed. Try to sleep.*

He slides into bed and allows himself to relax. As the night goes on, Walter finds himself dreaming of running a marathon. He speeds past his competition, sweat runs down his face. In the distance he sees it, the finish line is dead ahead. Each step is determined to reach it. It grows by the second, he gets closer and closer. With ease, he reaches first place and thinks, *Just a little more.*

Walter feels his feet sink. His eyes shoot down, he's running or rather *attempting* to run across thick mud. The track disappears, and he's now in a vast swamp. The humidity carries the rank stench of rotting wood and fish. A moth flies to him, its errant flight pattern makes it difficult to track. It lands on Walter's hand, he stares at the grayish walnut-brown thing. Its large black eyes pierce right through Walter.

A strange wave of emotions strikes at him, his heart races, palms sweat, and mouth dries up. The furry creature cleans its antenna and smiles at him. The sinister smile reveals serrated teeth. Walter swipes the aberration away, he fights the mud holding his feet hostage. He pulls and pulls eventually freeing himself. He bolts in the opposite direction taking large strides. Each stride is a huge struggle.

"Where is it you think you are going, Walter?" The familiar corrosive voice asks. "You cannot escape. Now, awaken!" Walter opens his eyes, gasping for air, and swinging away. His fists slam twice against a fuzzy wall, something wraps around his wrists stopping his frantic attempt at attacking. "Why fight, Walter? The difference in power is ridiculous. Honestly, can you travel across dimensions? No, you cannot!"

At that moment the darkness breaks in two places. A pair of crimson eyes peer at Walter.

His blood chills, and he freezes unable to think. The creature's weight shifts forward from Walter's legs to his chest. Sweat rolls down his forehead and neck as he feels the air being squeezed out of him. He then remembers the guard outside his room. He shouts as best as he can, "Help!"

A second passes, but the guard doesn't enter. The creature laughs and says, "Oh my dear Walter, scream all you want, no noise will escape this room." A bright white smile shines under the crimson eyes, even more darkness disappears revealing the creature's teeth. Rows and rows of small, pointed ivory daggers shine against the dim moonlight coming through the window.

Walter can barely make out the creature's outline. A pointed chin under a round head carrying a strange pair of leaf-shaped things overhead. *What are you?* he thinks.

"Your sculptor! That's what I am, Walter." The creature responds. It leans in close to Walter's face, smells Walter's neck, and whispers, "Your mind is still too strong, not malleable enough. I can fix this." The creature gently runs its long hand through Walter's hair, its eyes looking up as if feeling for something. "Found it!" The creature says as it plucks a small white light from Walter's mind.

Walter winces feeling a strange slither escape from his head. His stomach vibrates lightly.

"Enjoy your fading slumber, oh dear vessel." With a two-beat snap of its fingers, Walter loses consciousness.

CLICK. KTSS, KTSS, KTSS. The cassette's tape gets stuck after the button is pressed. Dr. Edwards slaps the recorder, setting the tape back in place. "This is Dr. Edwards recording patient log number four. The date is December fourth of 1998. Patient's name is Walter Rogers, patient number forty-one. Undiagnosed, however he experiences nightly hallucinations and a worsening anxiety. Walter, my notes say you haven't slept much since our last session. What's going on?"

Walter's eyes are half open and staring ahead. He says nothing. The doctor snaps his fingers near Walter's ear making him jump. "Huh? What happened?" Walter asks.

"Hi, Walter, we're in the middle of a session. Why can't you sleep well?" The doctor asks as he writes: *Patient is sleep deprived.*

Walter shakes his head. He sighs and says, "I, um, I don't know. My mind just won't relax. My—" *SLAM!* Walter strikes the table at full force, he keeps his palm pressed against it as he waits for the flaming sensation to dissipate from his hand. With anticipation, he stares at his hand as he slowly lifts it. "Fucking hell! I missed it again." He shouts, wiping his sweaty face.

"Missed? There's nothing there Walter." The doctor explains. He writes down more notes and continues, "What is it that you see, Walter?"

With a deep scoff he replies, "Moths! They're everywhere, can't you see?" He points up at the corners of the room.

Dr. Edwards looks around and writes: *Patient seems to be experiencing hallucinations at this moment. If they are from sleep deprivation or not, has yet to be determined.* Clearing his throat, he says, "When did you start to see these moths? And what do they do exactly?"

Walter keeps looking around the room, his shoulders slumped as his back curves forward. He faces the doctor explaining, "It started after I saw it again."

"The creature that's been visiting you?"

"Yes! Keep up."

"So the medication isn't working at all? You don't see any difference?"

"No, it's real! It's not in my head. It touches me!"

"Wasn't a guard placed outside your room for protection?"

"Yes but somehow that *thing* ... it has a way of controlling everything or everyone." Walter gets real close to Dr. Edwards, the nurse standing by the door steps forward, but Dr. Edwards stops him with a subtle hand gesture. Walter whispers, "I'm trying to figure out what it is, but it won't say. I only get cryptic answers from it."

"Cryptic how, Walter? Can you give me an example? I want to help you." Dr. Edwards replies, guiding Walter back to his seat.

"It said it's my sculptor. That I'm a vessel or something? Claims to be able to travel across dimensions. No, don't look at me like that! I know how insane I sound. You asked."

Dr. Edwards stops writing and says, "I'm not saying anything, Walter. All I'm doing is listening. What you're saying is helpful, in fact, I'm relieved to hear that you know that what you are saying is impossible. That's a sign that you are able to rationalize things through. That you aren't confusing reality with fantasy. That's a good thing. Look, mental issues are more difficult to treat than physical ones. They take time and effort on both sides. Now, returning to the creature. Have you seen it clearly? I haven't heard you describe it."

Walter lowers himself in his seat. He shakes his hands as if swatting away bugs. "No, not really. The room is too dark to see. I can barely make out a silhouette. It's not like us. It's ... I'm not sure how to explain it. I'm certain it's not human. Humanoid, yes but not human. I do know that."

Dr. Edwards nods, he tears a sheet of paper from his notebook and hands it to Walter. "Why don't you try to draw it for me?"

Walter takes the paper and starts sketching. A few minutes later, he hands the sketch to Dr. Edwards. "I know what it looks like. Keep an open mind," he begs.

Dr. Edwards inspects the sketch and writes: *The creature the patient sees is certainly in his head.* "Okay Walter, um, I want you to know that I'm here to help you. I'm going to prescribe you some sleeping pills and since you are still seeing the creature, I'll have you stop taking the anti-psychotics. It can interfere with the sleeping pills. Let's try something, try to get a good look at it, and try having a conversation with it. Stand up to it. I'll see you next week and hopefully, I'll get more information about it from you," he says extending his hand to Walter.

Walter sighs and shakes Dr. Edwards' hand. "Fine. But what happens if it gets angry?"

"I don't know, Walter. It hasn't hurt you yet, right? Besides, if you're a *vessel*, then you're important, meaning it likely won't hurt you." Dr. Edwards stands up as Walter is escorted out. He takes another look at the sketch and shakes his head. He places the sketch with the rest of his notes.

―᎒᎒―

Walter rests his head on the pillow. He clears his mind and waits for the medication to take effect. He turns away from the clock on his nightstand, pulling the covers over his head for at least some sense of security. The weight of his body becomes noticeable and heavy. His eyes close without permission, but he doesn't fight it, he accepts the feeling.

Walter finds himself walking through a wheat field. The golden sun shines above. He lets himself roam around, the wheat brushes against him like large bristles. The open sky carries a single white cloud, fluffy and light. The wheat sways from side to side following the breeze. It parts the wheat, revealing a pathway. *What's this?* Walter follows his curiosity.

The path is narrow, he walks for a few yards until the path takes him left. He turns and continues forward, the gold-soaked sunlight sinks into the horizon. A titanium crescent moon shines its cold light over the deep indigo veil of night. The pearlescent stars blink in a faded green hue, the rhythm almost identical to the green-banded broodsac feeding off a poor snail. Something about that pulsing makes Walter stop dead in his tracks.

A shiver slithers up his spine, and a rustling behind him shoots him forward deeper into the unknown path. He runs through the path, looking back by instinct. His eyes catch a dashing blur dive into the thick of the wheat from behind him. Walter speeds up, his breathing shallows. The rustling grows close, and a faint flutter comes from his right.

Something crashes against his face, it's so small it bounces right off. A second one crashes, then another ... and another. What were small weightless things, are now a swarming wave of fuzzy, fluttering moth-like things. The swarm surrounds Walter, he's vibrating from their incessant fluttering. He shuts his eyes and continues running. He swats the entire bunch away. All he hears is the roaring flutter of wings surging from behind him like a tsunami's wave.

The wave starts pushing back despite Walter's attempt at running through it. A sharp prickling spreads around Walter's body, like miniature hooks pulling his skin. He continues on as the hooks start reeling him in. The prickling turns into a full-on stinging. The feeling of fire covers Walter from head to toe.

He opens his mouth and prepares to unleash a piercing shriek. Only silence emerges from him. The fluttering wave lifts him up to the sky, the hooks buried in him pull at the limit of his skin. He tries to scream again only for his voice to get tangled up in his vocal chords. The skin from his back stretches and burns until it snaps. The roaring flutter fades away as he plummets back to the wheat field.

The wind blows directly into his lungs. The ground gets closer and closer until *SLAM!* The impact wakes Walter.

"Good, you're up," the creature's rotting voice says from behind Walter. "We have work to do."

A heavy pressure on Walter's back pins him down to his bed. "Get off me!" Walter shouts, his body twisting and trying to turn around.

The creature grabs Walter by the head, pulling back. Its long hand wraps almost completely around it. "Tsk, tsk, tsk. You do not give orders around here. Learn your place, *vessel*." The creature's free hand probes inside Walter's mouth. Unnaturally long digits feel around like an errant tarantula. The fine fur covering them rubs off lodging themselves in Walter's throat.

Two fingers latch themselves around the back of Walter's mouth. His throat spasms in bursts of threes as it tries to expel the intrusive hair. "Sit still, it'll be over soon." With a twist, a shooting pain runs through Walter's jaw. His back arches, he screams as the warm taste of fresh blood hits his tongue. The creature's hand leaves him, it has claimed its treasure. It gets off Walter and stands at the foot of the bed.

Walter immediately covers his mouth, he turns to it asking, "What did you do?"

Through the darkness, the garnet gaze gets close to Walter. "You know exactly what I did. A punishment for your childlike behavior. Negative reinforcement is how you humans learn." The ghastly white glow of its razor-ridden maw illuminates its hand. For the first time Walter sees something of the creature in detail. A long grayish artichoke green *Dalí-esque* hand with seven digits holding up a bloody molar. "You'll never understand the importance of this seemingly ordinary tooth. To our kind—it's priceless. Yet you self-sabotaging apes leave them to rot!"

Its hand wraps around Walter's neck pushing him back against the wall. The window lets in the dim moonlight hitting the creature's face. It pulls back, leaving Walter with a brief glimpse. He grabs the thing's hand and pries it back. *Shit!* Cold sweat runs down his face and his body acts out of horror. His arm swings forward letting out the strongest punch of his life.

The creature doesn't move, it simply stares at Walter. "You insignificant worm. You humans believe to be apex predators when in reality you are nothing more than a mite in *The Fountain's* hierarchy!" A two-beat snap paralyzes Walter, and it laughs like a blazing razor. "See? This weekly dance between us ... is just entertainment. Nothing more than playing with my prey. Disrespect won't be tolerated, your metamorphosis will be expedited. I've grown to like you, Walter, truly. Any requests before we start?"

Walter pays only half of his attention to what was just said, he's still trying to move. He looks at the creature's towering silhouette and tries replying only for his mouth to drool.

The creature smiles, picks Walter up with a single finger, and says, "No, dear Walter, your body is no longer yours. You are now part of something greater than yourself. We'll see each other one more time. Try to stay calm, for the larvae that is. In the meantime, keep your teeth clean. They'll be mine soon."

And with a wave of the creature's hand and Walter loses consciousness.

Dr. Edwards sits down placing his recorder on the desk. *CLICK*. Clearing his throat as the recorder starts, he begins, "This is Dr. Edwards recording patient log number sixteen. Today's date is December tenth of 1998. The patient's name is Walter Rogers. Patient number forty-one. Still undiagnosed yet worsening on a weekly basis. All his tests keep coming back normal. His hallucinations are still present, medication did not lessen them, and his anxiety has worsened significantly. Antipsychotics have been suspended indefinitely. Walter, I see here on my notes that you lost a tooth. What happened?"

Walter sits across from Dr. Edwards, his back arched forward, a quivering lip tries to get a message to Dr. Edwards, it fails before reaching the first syllable as a string of saliva stretches its way down to his lap. The cool liquid lands on his hand and slides between his fingers. He stares at Dr. Edwards, or so it seems. His eyes are fixed forward where, coincidentally, Dr. Edwards is sitting. Walter feels his eyes widen. He tries to open them more. He tries to get anyone's attention. *Help! I need help! I can't move!*

"Walter, can you speak for me? Tell me something. We had a plan, remember?"

Walter's eyes meet Dr. Edwards', who continues, "Walter speak, we've already had two other doctors take a look at you. There's nothing wrong with you besides the missing tooth, not physically anyway. The test results were normal." Turning to the nurse that brought Walter in, he asks, "Has he really not said anything since the last time I saw him?"

"Not a word," the nurse says. "Doesn't move either. I feel for him, we don't know if he can hear us or not."

I can hear you! I'm here! HELP!

Dr. Edwards jots down on his notes: *Walter Rogers, non-responsive since December fifth*. "Alright then, get him to his room then."

No, wait! WAIT!

The nurse grabs Walter's wheelchair and starts taking him back. As they reach Walter's room, the nurse parks the wheelchair beside the bed, "Alright Walter, I'll be back to check on you in half an hour. I left the TV on for you." Walter doesn't respond, he sits there, motionless until dinner time. He just stares at the TV, the cooking channel plays nonstop. The nurse returns with Walter's food. He sits down and starts feeding Walter. "Today we have roast beef and creamed spinach. For dessert there was jello, but I know you don't like it, so I snuck into the kitchen and got you some butterscotch pudding. I've seen you eat two of those before so I know you like it."

Walter does nothing, he hears everything, he's a hostage to his body. His week has been a living nightmare. At eight-thirty, the same kind nurse tucks Walter into bed. He shuts the lights off and leaves after saying goodnight. Walter stares at the ceiling, sleep eludes him. After spending the entire week locked inside his body, his eyes move. His thoughts are his only companions. *Finally! At least I can move something.* He has started to analyze everything in an attempt to keep his sanity as intact as possible. *When are you getting here?*

A few hours pass by, the night is silent like it usually is. His eyes have now adjusted to the darkness. Most things are somewhat visible. He stares at the door. *A dark rectangle with a silver circle. Why is it like that? It's due to the moonlight touching it from hundreds of thousands of miles away. Sounds so odd, like the moon was aiming. Funny.*

"*Interesting*, not funny," the eerie sharpness slices through the silence. "It starts now, Walter. Tonight you will achieve your purpose!" From underneath Walter, the creature reaches out and over the bed. A spidery hand pulls his mouth open while the other gestures above it. A strange rumbling starts somewhere deep inside Walter's gut. "Tonight," the voice says, "you will fulfill your destiny! A perfect vessel for the next horde!" The creature's voice emerges from the left, Walter looks left and sees the darkness moving.

The intense crimson eyes over a bone-white sea of pointed teeth is clearly visible through the veil of night. *What are you?* Walter tries to move, a futile attempt, but he keeps trying. His body knows how to move yet declines the order to do so, as if not ready to do so. He can feel his body wanting to move. The creature walks—no, hovers—over to him while staying upright, like a specter. The rumbling grows stronger.

"Knowing will not help. More often than not, knowledge becomes the gateway to endless questions. The more answers one has, the less one truly knows," a harassing caress across Walter's face chills his blood. The corrupted smile gets closer and closer as tears start pouring down Walter's eyes. "You deserve to know. After all, this is where we part ways. You humans have called my kind many things. None are accurate, though we agreed to go by the term *fairies*. We come from another dimension, one of much higher frequency than this immensely dense one. We've had to do some business with your species. But none like you, no, the special humans. The *casters*. Enough of this, it's irrelevant now. Let us begin the spawning!"

The rumbling stops altogether, a build-up of pressure inside Walter's guts expands until *POP!* Walter breaks free from his lethargic state with an ear-splitting shriek. His body twisting like a dug-up earthworm. Countless needle pricks start traveling Walter's insides. The rumbling is now an unmistakable fluttering. The creature applauds, his haunting smile dripping with corrosive pride.

It begins making intricate hand gestures while murmuring in a harsh blunt tongue. Walter starts to float up to the nearest corner of the ceiling. The pain robs him of any kind of control over his body. Unable to breathe, his bladder along with his other sphincters, force themselves open in a desperate attempt to inhale. The stench of urine and feces invade the small room.

The creature pulls an ever-long silver strand from its unholy maw, flinging it at Walter. The endless string wraps around poor Walter, eventually encasing and anchoring him in a silvery silk-like cocoon to the upper corner of his room. His pain-filled shouts are now muffled by his new *bedding*. The creature cuts the silk strand and sighs from satisfaction. It takes a moment to admire its craftsmanship. Walter's eyes are the only part of him not encased by the cocoon.

The creature flicks the lights on, revealing its true form for Walter to witness. A towering grayish artichoke green moth-like abomination standing nearly ten feet tall. Its four wings wrap it neatly resembling a fur cape fit for royalty. Around its long slender neck, it wears a golden necklace adorned with what looks like human teeth. It waves at Walter, the unnaturally long hand has seven fingers, two of them being thumbs. "I thank you, Walter, your sacrifice means the survival of the kingdom. Now come, my children!"

Walter's eyes bulge out as tears are running down in streams, the tears begin turning red, and from his eyes, a swarm of miniature fairies claw and bite their way out. His muted screams are interrupted by a thick gurgling. Seconds later, the tiny monsters burst forth from every direction: mouth, ears, nose, and presumably his genitals. The silver cocoon becomes tainted in a rich shades of red, yellow, and brown. The last thing Walter sees as he bleeds out, is the swarm of creatures as they leave through a deep yellow portal in the wall.

The next day, the morning nurse arrives, opens Walter's door, and screams in terror. Two more nurses run in, one freezes while the other joins in adding to the chaotic screaming. The image of Walter's remains—dangling from the stained cocoon like the leftovers from a giant bird-eating spider—now forever branded in their brains, it bides its time for the perfect moment to reappear randomly in their dreams.

The official report determined the cause of death to be a sudden heart attack. The nurses that found him were forced to sign a nondisclosure agreement. The autopsy results showed something ate him from the inside out, leaving only bones inside a flimsy sack of skin like a collapsed tent. The biggest mystery of all...why would the predator need its prey's teeth?

TIMMY IS BACK

by Jose Francisco Trevino Chavez

Tim stands and leaves before the burial ends. He swore only two things could bring him back to this god-forsaken place. An apology, or their death. He hears the town's murmurs. He can also feel several judgmental eyes on his back, but he doesn't care.

I should, but I don't. I can't, especially after how they chose to end things.

Kicking out their only son, leaving him at his own devices at sixteen. Who does that? *Monsters*, that's who.

Just before he reaches the rental car that brought him to this dying cemetery, he's intercepted by a familiar face. Last time they were together, they were at each other's throats. Now he's smiling at Tim in a semi-formal blue suit.

"Hi, Tim," his cousin says. "I'm sorry for your loss. I hate to see you, given the circumstances."

"Hello, Oscar. I'd thank you, but I know you. What do you want?"

Oscar smiles and says, "Oh come on, man. We were close once. *Really* close. Then you left and look at you now." He looks Tim up and down. "You look great in your marine uniform."

"I'm in the Navy. I'm not a Marine."

Striking his forehead with his palm, Oscar replies, "I always mix them up. Look, um..."

"Spit it out or I leave," Tim blurts out.

"Okay, okay, fine. I do want something. I know you hate this town and knowing you, you'll leave ASAP. I'm a realtor, and I assume you want to sell your folks' house, right?"

Tim nods, "Yes, I just need to clear it out first. Congratulations, dip-shit, we have a deal. You know the address. Drop by whenever." Before Oscar can say anything else, Tim gets inside his rental car and peels out of the cemetery.

He arrives at his childhood home a few minutes later, parks, and sits there staring at the two-story house without a thought in his mind.

After god knows how long, Tim snaps out of his trance to find himself with a death grip on the steering wheel. The urge to piss forces him out of the car and into the house. He struggles with the locked door, and for some reason, he gets a flashback to last week.

He's brought back to the coroner's office, where he identified the dead couple as his parents. Seeing them lying on the cold steel table sent shivers down his back. Their emaciated bodies made them look so old it reminded Tim of Holocaust victims. They carried anxiety and pain in their faces, all twisted and weathered. Despite the relationship between Tim and his parents, seeing them like that brought nothing but regret and emptiness.

Shaking his head, Tim regains focus and enters the house. Despite it being 11 a.m., the house is dark. Taking a whiff, he smells the dust and loneliness within. He runs past the living room and turns left before entering the kitchen and reaching the restroom. The silence of the house is completely out of character from what Tim remembers. Most of his memories are overflowing with noise.

His father yelling at the TV either because his team was losing or he disagreed with the ref. His mother constantly complaining about the sports-related yelling, which turned into an argument Tim is still convinced the neighbors could overhear. After they finished biting each other's head off, a brief moment of silence always followed. The calm before the storm. That silence never lasted. Its brief nature was always snuffed out by the near-pornographic sounds that bled through the thin walls of their bedroom and into Tim's.

The violent flush brings the house back from the dead, if only for a second. Afterward, he heads to the kitchen and peeks into the fridge. *How is it completely empty?* Closing the fridge in defeat, he orders a pizza. Thirty-five minutes later, Tim is munching on a warm slice of Hawaiian pizza, wandering the house.

Nothing changed in fifteen years, really? Tim thinks as he sees the same decor. He enters his mother's home office. Images of her dismissing him as she typed flicker through so quickly they resemble a strobe light. He looks around and sees what's on her desk. A laptop from a few years ago under a thin veil of dust, two notebooks, and a few balled-up sheets of paper.

Tim looks inside one of the notebooks. Scribbles and scraps of ideas are all he sees. He puts it down and continues to the bookshelf behind him. Tons of books from every genre possible, most of which Tim doesn't recognize. His finger bounces from spine to spine. It stops bouncing and Tim pulls out a book he hasn't seen since he left. Wrapping his grease-covered fingers around it, he opens it to his favorite spot. Chapter five of Mary Shelley's *Frankenstein* has always fascinated him.

Tim slides his maroon eyes across the page and a smile forms the instant he reads the monster's description. Hollywood has the habit of botching book adaptations and this one is no exception; green is the color they chose. The vivid parakeet-green popped out from the silver screen back in the days of the dawn of color cinema, but it doesn't compare to the book.

The book's description of the monster was and forever will be a grim and grotesque analogy of the horror of birth. Dull yellow and watery eyes on shriveled yellow skin that hid no muscle from sight, lustrous black hair and stark black lips. A live being that resembles death; how can an angst-filled teenager not fall in love with that description?

FEAR

DING-DONG! The book drops as the unexpected ring nearly separates his body and soul. Tim makes his way to the front door.

On the other side is Oscar with paperwork and a camera. "Hey Tim, I figured I'd take the outside pictures first and when I finish, you could answer any questions about the house. Cool?"

"Sure. I'll leave the door unlocked. Let me know if you need anything," Tim says before shutting the door. He returns to the kitchen and continues eating while reading *Frankenstein*. One pizza slice turns to two, then three, and finally four. Tim leaves the remaining pizza for dinner later. He drags himself to the living room and drops onto the couch, the weight of his eyelids growing to unimaginable proportions before he succumbs and falls asleep.

A gentle tap on Tim's boots wakes him up. Oscar waves and says, "I'm sorry for waking you, but I'm finished taking pictures. I can come back tomorrow if you're too tired."

"No, let's get this over with."

"Okay, I think the kitchen lights are better," Oscar comments, leading Tim to the kitchen.

Tim accepts a folder with a questionnaire about the house. As he fills out the paperwork, Oscar excuses himself to take a phone call outside. The questionnaire takes a while. By the time he's finished, his stomach demands his attention. He hands the folder back to Oscar and tells him, "Alright, man. I'm done. What's next?"

"I'll post the pictures online and see if people are interested. If they are, I'll call you to see when I can show them the house in person. Sound good?"

"Sure. Let me give you my number," Tim writes his number on the folder and Oscar hands him a business card.

"I'll get out of your hair then. It's getting late."

"Yeah, I'm starving," Tim says, turning to the box of leftover pizza.

"Thanks for the opportunity. I'll let myself out," Oscar replies.

Tim is too busy already tasting his pizza to reply. He flips the lid open, but the box is empty. *What the hell*. He immediately makes his way to the front door and stops Oscar just as he is about to leave. "You ate my pizza while I slept? What's wrong with you?"

"What are you talking about?"

"Quit the crap. I had four slices of Hawaiian pizza left on the kitchen counter. You saw the box. Why didn't you ask for a slice?"

"That's impossible, Tim."

"Oh, screw you! This is exactly like the time you left your weed here. You let me take the blame, knowing how my parents were!"

"Tim! I'm allergic to pineapple! If I had had a single piece, I'd be dying!"

Tim steps back and stops for a second. "Yeah, I remember now. I'm sorry. I—I don't know what happened. I lost my head for a second. I—"

"It's fine. You must've eaten it and forgot. Look, you're stressed. I get it. We're cool. Oh, by the way, I'm sorry for your loss. I heard how they found your parents. It's awful."

Tim nods. "Thanks. Honestly, I'm confused about the whole thing. The coroner couldn't explain how my parents ended up like that. I'll see you soon."

Oscar nods right back. His gaze holds on to Tim's, as silence fills the air. "Not even an inkling? I mean there's got to be a reason."

"No. Not a clue." Tim begins shutting the door but Oscar doesn't move.

"I can't imagine how you must've felt seeing them like that."

A heavy sigh escapes Tim's lips, he opens his mouth only to close it a second later.

"You're tired. I'll let you to it then. I'll see you soon." Oscar steps back and out of the house.

Tim slowly shuts the door. He stands there for a moment trying to remember how many slices he ate. After the fifth failed attempt, he gives up.

I'll just order another pizza.

Thirty minutes later, his new pizza has arrived. After eating half of it and taking a picture to prove it, he puts it away and hovers in the doorway.

Quit stalling and go to bed. You're tired.

He heads upstairs and hopes his parents hadn't touched his old room. On the last step, his foot catches the lip, sending him sprawling forward. He catches himself before hitting the floor and breathes out before continuing. He turns right and sees the door to his room but hesitates as his hand hovers over the knob. He closes his eyes and swings the door open.

When he opens them, he's brought back to September of 2009, the day Tim was kicked out. He shakes his head, willing the memory away.

Didn't touch a thing. Lucky me.

His old posters were still holding up on the wall above his bed. He walks around the room and feels a strange tightness swelling inside him. He stops at his desk and sees an old sketchbook. He'd spent countless hours drawing in it.

He runs his fingers across the dusty cover and bumps the pencil on it. It rolls off the desk and under his bed. From underneath the bed, roll out three crayons: red, blue, and yellow. When Tim kneels and begins picking them up, he takes a look under his bed, looking for the pencil. There, he sees a journal he doesn't recognize. He pulls it out and inspects it while sitting on the edge of his bed.

Was this mine?

The cover is blank. He opens it and begins reading the text written in blue crayon.

December 8th, 1998 Log #1
I've gone unnoticed for three days and have survived on nothing but scraps of food and cat food. The couple suspects nothing, however, I believe their child senses my presence. He seems to be about four years old. For reasons I can't understand, the child waves at me through the air ducts despite covering myself in complete shadows. Humans are

supposed to have terrible night vision. This won't stop me from feeding properly. I must sedu—

———ele———

Tim jumps to his feet and throws the journal across the room. His hands shake uncontrollably as he looks above the door to the air duct. The duct holds the expected amount of darkness and nothing more. He remembers waving at the ducts but never knowing why.

That was real? No, no, no. Think this through. Mom would often write odd ideas like this. This must have been written by her. Relax, Tim.

He forces his shoulders down and sits back in his bed. With his eyes still nailed to the journal, a few seconds struggle by before Tim can bear it no more. He jumps out of bed and picks the journal back up. He opens it and continues reading a few pages in.

———ele———

April 15, 2001 Log #9

Timmy was playing with his cousin during the Easter egg hunt this morning. I watched from his bedroom window. The parents supervised from a distance. As the children were searching, I couldn't keep my eyes off Timmy. I wanted to get a closer look, so I snuck out to the backyard while everyone ate. I hid inside a bush near one of the eggs. Eventually, Timmy found the egg near me. I watched through the leaves. I was so close I could've touched him.

I held my breath as he walked away with a smile. Then I returned to his bedroom. He might have caught me watching for a second from his bedroom window just before they finished the search. I'm not sure how much he saw or understood. The cat no longer wanders the house at night; not since we met last month.

Her fear is delicious.

Tim slams the journal shut. He turns to the window and closes his eyes as his mind throws him to that day. He can still smell the burgers cooking on his father's propane grill. The cool breeze swaying the grass in the backyard. Those colorful eggs, one under the hose, another by the shed, and his favorite one hidden between the garden gnomes his mother brought a few weeks before.

One of the few pleasant childhood memories he has held onto, now morphs. It changes like a body changes with cancer. It twists and corrupts itself with one detail, a detail Tim had forgotten over time. From the corner of his eye, he saw a figure. It was just a second, but he knew he'd seen something. It was iron-gray with large yellow eyes. Of course, when he turned back, the figure was gone.

Tim's eyes spring open. He hadn't thought about that figure in nearly twenty years.

No, no. It can't be, can it?

Rushing to his feet, he paces his room from corner to corner. He feels the air thin out and his chest clenches. He stops immediately and says, "Talk it out. You're trained for this, remember? There's no danger, it's anxiety."

With short, shallow breaths, Tim begins. He holds his breath for ten seconds, then releases it slowly. Repeating until he resumes breathing normally. A few minutes pass while he regains focus.

You told Mom about that thing that night. So she knew, meaning that the journal is probably one of those weird writing projects.

With a sigh of relief, he says, "Relax, Tim. Being here is fucking with your head."

Like a log, he falls to his bed. Before he knows it, he's asleep.

The creaking of the wooden floors wakes him. He turns to the hall, expecting either of his parents. Reality returns to his hazy-still-half-asleep brain, and an uncomfortable pressure in his lower abdomen gets his attention. He drags himself out of bed and walks down the hallway to the upstairs bathroom. Despite not having been here since the age of sixteen, his muscle memory is still reliable enough to lead him through the dark.

The sudden cold from the tiled floor tells him he's reached the bathroom. He continues forward; each passing second fills his bladder drop by drop. He hurries forward with his hands out in front to prevent any unwanted collisions, the pressure in his bladder now starting to become a problem.

Come on. Where's the toilet?

With squinting eyes, he sees a never-ending black hallway. *The hell?*

Tim stops and feels along the wall, looking for the light switch. With a flick of his finger, light assaults his eyes like the powerful explosion of a flashbang. He clenches his eyes shut and waits for them to adjust to the light before slowly opening them up. His groggy dream-haze vanishes with his gasp. His eyes are wide, refusing to blink as if forcing Tim to see the horror before him.

The small bathroom of his childhood home where there was barely enough space for a single person, is no more. He is standing in a narrow and long corridor-like restroom. The toilet waits for him about twenty feet ahead under a badly placed air vent. A strange echo coming from the vent steals his attention from the illogical dimensional change. His eyes shift up to the vent. The vent is wide open, its insides hold nothing but darkness save for that sound.

Tim takes one step forward, paying close attention to the echo. The airy sound repeats itself with a rhythm. *Sounds like... a chuckle?* Tim stares at the darkness of the vent. His gaze latches on for several seconds. *SLAM!* The vent shuts itself, sending Tim back with a flinch. The shift of his weight sends Tim falling straight on his ass.

The long corridor of a restroom is gone. In its place is the same bathroom Tim had expected moments before. He rubs his eyes once, then twice, but nothing changes. The bathroom is exactly as it should be. A fatigued sigh escapes Tim's lips and says, "You're half-asleep, just piss and go to bed."

Tim returns to his bedroom with an empty bladder. The lack of energy makes his body feel heavier than it is. He covers himself in his sheets and closes his eyes, fighting exhaustion.

What happened back there?

The more he thinks about it, the more questions appear.

Was it a dream? It had to be. Things don't just change out of the blue. Do they? Go to sleep, Tim.

Several tosses and turns later, Tim opens his eyes and stares at the ceiling. The incident in the bathroom replays itself in his head. He sighs and admits to himself that he's not sleeping tonight. Turning to his nightstand, he takes his phone, checking the time. 3:05 a.m. He unlocks his phone and dives into his Instagram feed.

He's met by the black reflection of his face. He refreshes the app, but nothing. His eyes hover on the upper right-hand corner.

No signal? No Wi-Fi either? How?

Tim sits up and walks around his old room with his phone raised up high.

Still no signal?

Lowering his phone in defeat, he sits on the edge of the bed until he remembers he saw the router in his mom's office and heads straight to it.

He flicks the lights on and walks down the stairs, turning right and heading to the back of the house. He enters the office and there it is. Through the darkness, the little green lights flicker, accompanied by a single red light. The light above comes on, and Tim kneels down to inspect the problem.

Everything is plugged in. No visible damage to the router itself. Let's see the cables.

He runs his hands behind and down the machine into the snake-like nest of cables. Something frayed collides with the tip of his fingers. He grabs it and pulls it out. His face scrunches up as he sees the cable has been ripped apart. "What the fuck?"

He tosses the cable back in frustration and heads back to his room, dragging himself up the stairs, each step landing heavily with anger. On the last step, his foot misses the distance, stubbing his toe, "Shit!" He falls to his knees and, after a few seconds of pain, crawls into his room. The strange crayon-written journal is the first thing he sees as he enters the room. He stares at it, takes it, and flips it open in an attempt to distract the pain away.

This time, the text is a vivid orange.

September 30, 2004 Log #20

Things have been slow. Tim's parents are disappointed with his grades. Tutoring isn't helping much. His mother constantly checks up on him while he's doing homework. It's annoying to just watch him. It's boring. If he's not drowning in homework, he's on his little video game thing.

On the other hand, his parents stress him so much that his dreams are so filling. I love this home environment. A barely present accountant father glued to the television, an uptight mother of a writer whose concentration is weaker than wet paper with a tendency to scream her frustrations out on whoever is near, and a compliant little boy with constant nightmares. The best part is that his mind has developed a slight tear, allowing me to slip into his dreams. I usually watch from afar until I strike, shaped like a mangled scarecrow.

Tim looks up from the journal, his face is twisted and sweaty.

This story is dark, really dark. Even for her. Exposing my nightmares for money? Is this really Mom? I mean... who else could it be, right?

Tim scratches his head and hesitates to continue reading. His morbid curiosity defeats him as he flips through the pages.

January 14, 2007 Log #28

I missed an entire month. I was unable to document my progress due to a change of plans. Tim is now thirteen, and I can smell his hormones fluctuating throughout the day. He's developing nicely. His parents are constantly fucking after every fight. This doesn't help. His scent drives me insane. It's intoxicating. He'll be ready in no time. His mother is struggling with work, so naturally I took advantage. While she wasn't in her office, I searched up typical porn a teenage boy would like. The moment she saw the search history on her computer... She turned into a true banshee. By the time she finished, poor little Timmy cried himself to sleep. His—

Tim stops reading before finishing the entry. A heavy pressure fills the air.

How could she know I cried that night?

Pacing back and forth in his room, he tries to remember that next day, but everything is hazy. Too faded to trust. "You must have told her at some point," he says to calm himself. "Except you know you never told her." After saying that, Tim feels his tongue stick to the roof of his mouth. He runs it against his inner cheek; the texture is like sandpaper. It scratches every nook and cranny.

Tim exits his room and walks downstairs and to his right into the kitchen. He pulls the fridge open. The light escapes, illuminating the white interior. A cold veil of air wraps Tim as he sees the deserted interior. A defeated sigh is followed by, "Right, you're empty for some fucking reason." He takes his only option left, the faucet. He turns it on and dives into the running stream. The cool water running down his throat revives the inside of his mouth.

He heads back down the hallway toward the stairs only to somehow walk into the kitchen from the right. It shouldn't be possible. A quick turn back shows Tim the hallway to the back of the house. The same one leading to the restroom and his mother's office. He flips the lights on, looks down the hall, and can clearly see the bottom of the stairs. Without overthinking it, Tim walks down the hall.

The lights flicker, Tim's stomach turns, and vertigo sets in. His weight shifts to the side, forcing Tim to grab the wall. The flickering continues, and reality turns into a crude flip book of pictures of his home's hallway. The vertigo disappears just before the lights finally stop their flickering. Tim's vision adjusts to the light showing him standing at the back of the kitchen. A burst of sweat covers him as his stomach implodes.

No, how did…?

The lack of sense forces Tim to sit down. He presses firmly on his temples. He focuses on the cold tiles stealing body heat from his ass.

Five, four, three—
SLAM!

The explosive sound makes him jump to his feet. He looks around, searching for the culprit.

No broken windows, dishes, or anything out of place.

Tim deflates against the kitchen island and finds the journal waiting for him. It's open; its cream pages and crayon text demand for him to continue reading. Tim reels back from shock. He bolts to the front door, and each sock-lined footstep slides on the floor, threatening to trip him the entire way.

He grips the doorknob, turns it, and yanks. The front yard is nowhere in sight. Tim is instead greeted by the inside of a house. Down and near the back, he can see a man standing from behind. The man's clothes seem so familiar. Tim turns back around and runs past the kitchen and into the last hallway where he sees a man standing at the end of the hall, just like before. Only this time, he's looking back, exactly like Tim.

Oh fuck! That's—that's me!

He slams the door and stumbles back.

Tim's mind goes into overdrive, sending aimless thoughts and incomplete ideas nowhere useful. He turns back and forces himself to look down the hallway toward the back of the house in search of the *other* Tim. This time, Tim seems to be alone. He slowly turns back to the door but stops himself from reaching out.

He turns to the window and reaches for it. His fingers frantically grope at the latch. The tips of his fingers slide past the latch once, twice, three times. He kneels down for a closer look. The latch, window frame, and pane are painted on the wall. "No. No! NOOO!"

A twisted version of the classic gag from *The Looney Tunes* now holds him hostage. Tim turns around and presses his back against the wall, his senses lit on fire.

This can't be! You know this house! There's supposed to be a way out!

Tim bounces his eyes around in search of an answer that simply isn't there. The empty living room is exactly as it should be. The stairs seem normal. The hallway to the kitchen is just like any other hallway. The kitchen has nothing out of the ordinary.

The journal in the kitchen—that's it! That's what's different!

He marches back to the kitchen, his eyes locked onto the journal. He stares at it without missing a second. It's almost as if he expects the journal to move. Several seconds crawl by before Tim growls, "Ugh! What's going on? What are you?" A mix of rage and fear seeps out of him as he takes a kitchen knife to the journal's cover. He stops just before he can cut into it. "You have to have some sort of answers." He swipes the journal off the kitchen island and takes it with him.

As he's walking upstairs, a creaking reaches him from behind. He stops immediately to listen.

It's the wood floor... it's gone.

He continues up a few steps before hearing it again.

It's back, but it sounds—closer?

Taking a quick peek over his shoulder, he catches something that stands his neck hairs on end. What seems like a grayish spider on the corner of the wall behind him, slides back into the darkness.

Tim darts off to the second floor, reaching his parents' room in record time. He slams the door shut behind him, locking it. A sharp pain climbs up his right hand; he looks down and realizes he's got a death grip on the journal. He pries his cramped hand off with his left.

What was that thing? Was that a hand? Wait, I've—I've seen it before!

Tim opens the journal, trying to remember the exact date. He flips through the pages, keeping in mind the year. The text is now a deep blue. A few pages in, it changes to a jade-green, then a cherry-red. He stops in 2010 and skims through the logs. "That's it," he whispers to himself.

May 29, 2010 Log #38

Today, my plan fell apart. My insides still twist as I write this. During lunchtime, I decided to push things. I had taken a few objects over the last three weeks. I started small. I moved things around to places they didn't belong. The car keys to the washing machine, some documents to the basement, etc.

Apparently, despite having unlikable parents, my Timmy... my beautiful Timmy still loves his parents and wants them to have a good marriage. I took a plum lipstick she didn't like and kissed her husband's shirt with the fullest and sexiest female lips I'm capable of making. The kiss stain was meant for her to find, not my Timmy! He confronted his father, and that imbecile of a brute made things worse. My Timmy lost his temper and punched his idiot father.

To make matters worse, that bitch defended her husband! What kind of mother does that? They kicked him out! I've lost my Timmy, and it's my fault! He was ready for me. From his bedroom window, I watched him leave with nothing more than his backpack and a gym bag full of clothes. He took a final look back; both of us were crying. I waved goodbye. I know he saw me. Even if it was just briefly, I know he saw. I took a form I knew he'd find pleasant. I don't know if I'll see him again. For now, I smell his bed. His scent still stirs me from within.

"I—I remember. The woman at my window—I remember her," Tim's words spill from his lips as that day replays itself for him. The scorching sun beating down on him as he wiped the tears from his face and that last glimpse at his home. Then, something moving from his room catches his attention. A naked, slender woman with dark gray skin and pale yellow eyes waving. Tim takes a second look only to find his curtains swaying from left to right.

Tim returns to the present, wondering so much. He continues reading.

December 23, 2010 Log #39

It's only been seven months since my Timmy was kicked out. How can I achieve my goal now? He was perfect! His parents are not ideal for my needs. Because of what happened, I can barely stand to look at his father. The mother isn't bad, a tad old for gestation, but she'll have to do, for now. As for him, he'll be my backup.

September 25, 2011 Log #42

I slowly started programming them both. During the night, I hang above them from the ceiling fan. Once they enter a deep sleep, I morph their dreams. For weeks now, all they dream of is sex. I have them come so close to reaching ecstasy. Just before they finish, I wake them, leaving them all pent up.

Today while the husband was away, I drained her energy. I whispered in her mind, leading her to the bedroom. She was mine in seconds. I fulfilled all her desires. Despite being under my hypnosis, she was quite responsive. Her body, scent, and moans were delightful. Feeding off her is so easy. She's a better lover than I gave her credit for.

Tim stops himself. His insides burn, and the internal inferno rises through him. He doesn't hold back and cries out, "What do you want from me?" He strikes at the wall only hurting himself. The electric protest coming from his hand's nerve endings ultimately defeats him, stopping him from any further violent outbursts. Leaning against the door, he slides to the floor.

From behind the door, a gentle scratching calls to him. Tim jumps to his feet and makes sure he's locked inside. Heavy panting followed by a gentle moan slides through the door into the room.

That voice, I've heard it before.

Tim remembers hearing that same moan in various dreams. "Leave me alone!" his faltering voice easily drowns out the haunting moans. His fear morphs. Fire runs through his veins, and he slams against the door, forcing it to rattle on its hinges.

Fleeing footsteps and creaky floorboards let Tim breathe again. He lets out a shuddering breath and falls to his knees.

You have to get out of here. But how? There's no front door and the windows are a lie!

"Think Tim, think," he tells himself. He begins turning the room upside down. From under the bed, in the closet, and in the dresser, he looks for something, anything that could help him. Alas, nothing useful is within grasp. He takes a look at the time on his phone, 2:14 a.m. He lies down across from the door and looks underneath it.

I don't see anything. Whatever that thing is. Does it even have feet?

He stops himself before the questions drive him mad. With no option left, Tim takes the journal and slowly cracks the door open.

He fights a shudder as he sees scratch marks on the door. Five claw marks dragged down from shoulder height down to possibly the waist. Besides them, a purple lipstick mark. Full lips painted on the door. "It's the same shade as—" Tim thinks out loud. He creeps over to the stairs and, at a snail's pace, walks down. Step after step, he goes, his breathing controlled, measured, and muted. The short trip down is uncomfortably elongated.

His posture weighs him down. His back and thighs tense up, and a lonesome bead of sweat runs down his face. He stops to check his cell reception.

No service. Wait, what? 2:10?

The stairs tilt down like shutters, changing into a steep ramp. His socks provide no traction at all, forfeiting him to gravity's pull. He slides down, and his phone falls into oblivion. He reaches in every direction, hoping to find the handrail. The trip takes turn after turn. Some are wide while others are sharp and narrow.

SLAM! CRASH! SMACK!

The slide from hell comes to a stop, sending Tim crashing against a wall. His head bounces off the floor, and everything is out of focus. He slowly sits up and sees where he is. "No! Let me go!" Tim screams from his room. Over and over, he pounds at the ground. A throat-ripping scream erupts from inside him, forcing him into a coughing fit.

From the hall, a gentle noise comes. "Shh," Tim hears. The pitch-black hall hides the creature completely. His imagination runs rampant as his eyes try to keep up, jumping from corner to corner despite seeing nothing there. The journal comes flying in, landing a few inches from him.

"You want me to keep reading? Why?" Tim's questions are unanswered by the void. The door shuts itself. "I'm not doing it!" he shouts. Tim sits there in the dark for a long while. His thoughts are the only things in his control. Time continues, and eventually, Tim feels hours have passed.

Just give up, there's no escape. None at a—
What? No! Why did I think that? I didn't, did I?
Yes, you did.

Tim slaps himself twice, "Get out of my head. Get out!" He stands up and shouts at the air vent, "Get out of my head!"

The journal flips open.

"I'm not reading!"

The journal slams shut. And then it opens again.

FEAR

"No!" On and on, the journal opens and closes. Every time it does, the sound grows louder and louder. Tim covers his ears and balls up in a corner. The sound of flapping paper digs into Tim's ears. It burrows itself down to the bone. "Stop it! Stop it! Stop it!" he begs to no avail. "Fine, I'll read! Just quit!"

The cacophony stops, and all noise levels plummet. A single page turns. It waits open for him right down the middle. His trembling hand reaches for it. The canary-yellow crayon writing is somehow visible through the darkness.

April 19, 2012 Log #44

Six months of having her and no sign of anything. I can only feed off her lust for so long. I don't understand why the seed won't take. I'll continue trying intermittently. The husband is primed and ready.

July 24, 2012 Log #45

For the past three months, I've been switching between mates. Despite the fact that I may never forgive myself for accidentally kicking my Timmy out of his home, his parents are not so bad in bed. Feels good to be the submissive one for a change. Timmy's father is strong... for a human. He knows how to keep going for a while. I expected him to get straight to the point and keel over beside me, but that's not the case.

He uses his weight to his advantage. I let him think he has full control over me. It gets me going. His brutish nature is fun. Unfortunately, despite having him almost every day, I still have yet to see his seed latch to me. I'll keep trying them both.

December 20, 2015 Log #86

Three years! Three years of wasted time and fruitless lust! Like animals in heat, that's how I've treated these useless creatures! And for what? No matter what I try, there's no pregnancy! I've made sure that all of us are still fertile, but for some unknown reason, I don't have any hatchlings yet! These under-evolved things are nothing but useless sex toys! I'll have to punish them for wasting my time.

Oh, my Timmy! How I wish you could be here. I never had the chance to touch you. Enjoy you. Savor you. Just from how you smelled back when we shared a room—I knew you were the one who could bring me to reproduce. Just remembering your scent, it gets me excited and ready. I'm salivating and sweating for you, my darling. Mark my words: I will have you!

February 20, 2017 Log #100

It's been a year since I stopped breeding with my toys. These last two months, I've been experimenting with something. I've only heard rumors of my kind being able to do so, but I didn't think it was possible. Time manipulation is draining and painful, but it's worth it knowing that they're losing their minds because of me. Their anguish feeds me much more than anything else they can offer.

Seeing how they feel a minute go by in more than an hour's time tastes exquisite! Their confusion, fear, and the best part... their anger! I let them go off at each other and when things start getting out of hand, I step in. I freeze them before the violence really starts and force them into heat for hours on end.

Tim peels his eyes off the journal. He looks up to the vents and despite not seeing anything, he asks, "I don't want to read this! What do you want from me?"

The room's silence carries Tim's answer. He lets go of the journal. The second he does, it snaps at him. Just like before, the journal frantically shuts. The snap catches Tim's finger, and a warm sting spreads across the tip. Looking down, Tim sees a crimson-red drop falling to the ground following the journal.

The darkness of the room is somehow repelled by the falling drop of fresh blood. An orb of liquid-red light. The small drop lands and spreads on a journal page. The red slowly crawls across the page. It gets absorbed by the yellowed page, turning the segment a burnt orange.

From the air vent above the door, a deep yet restrained moan shatters the seemingly solid silence. The low pitch of the moan carries across the room, slowly flooding it. Tim's skin crawls upon hearing it. His eyes shoot up to the vents, but the darkness reveals nothing to him. The air feels thick and hard to breathe in. His eyes stay fixed on the vents.

Where are you?

The book flaps twice, calling for him. Without looking away, Tim kneels down for the journal and continues reading.

September 28, 2019 Log #110

Manipulating time has become second nature to me now. I've now been starving my toys. Making them believe they just ate when they haven't seen more than a few bites for nearly two weeks. They're losing weight fast, and their stress levels are always rising. It feeds me. Keeps me young.

Now that they are always on the verge of losing their minds, their true colors are peeking out. My Timmy's mother, I caught her talking in her sleep. She mentioned him. My Timmy. Something about how she said his beautiful name... maybe it was the tone. Perhaps it was her twisted expression or the tears escaping her closed eyes. Her pain aroused me so. She said something about missing him. Oh, her anguish! It nourished me so much, I didn't need to eat in two days.

She'll worsen soon. So will he. Eventually, they'll break. They'll—

She thought about me?

Tim looks away from the journal. A slow pressure builds inside his chest. A gentle pout forms around Tim's lips.

She missed me?

Slowly, he covers his mouth and muffles his cries. His mother's face pops into his mind as his eyes close. Tears begin pouring down his face as it grows hot. Then, several moments flash by. Moments of her yelling at him, dismissing him, scolding him for no apparent reason. Now Tim can see his father too. His yelling is as loud and clear as the day he shouted at him. The countless insults and belittling. Then he's placed back to the last time he saw them. The lipstick stain on his father's shirt. His swings at his father.

The pain from that day appears again. The electricity running across his hand forces him to open his eyes. The origin of his pain is obvious now. A hole on the wall around the size of an orange stares Tim head-on.

It's not real. Snap out of it, Tim! Don't close your eyes. Can't trust your mind.

Tim looks down at his hand, finding his knuckles scraped and slightly peeled.

The journal starts snapping again. Before it can continue, Tim says, "Alright, alright!"

December 25, 2019 Log #111

I'm not sure if Timmy's mom has finally broken or if it's the time of year. She found my Timmy online and even found his phone number. Out of fear, she changed her phone number. She's been calling him every day this month, but my Timmy won't answer. I love how she had her hopes up all for nothing. Her husband keeps telling her it's a lost cause. He's recognized that they shouldn't have kicked him out, especially considering his age.

It serves them right. I'll never forgive them for that. Now that I know I'll never get a single offspring from either of them, my sole purpose for toying with them is to make sure they pay for what they did to my Timmy! At least their suffering feeds me. Once I drain them, I'll go looking for him.

Those calls—they were from her? Oh why, why didn't I answer?

Tim covers his face, remembering the calls from the unknown number so vividly. On the last two calls, he'd been so close to answering. Something in him wanted to answer, but he just didn't. Now, the bitter weight of regret is crushing him like the heavens on Atlas' shoulders.

"Why? I should have picked up!" Tim shouts. The walls echo back his frustration and rage. The echo grows louder and clearer. The words warp and the tone shifts to a mockery. Tim's words claw at him without a drop of mercy. "Stop it. Stop it! STOP IT!!!" Tim shouts through the supernatural echoes.

The room falls dead silent once more. The only thing he can hear is his heartbeat. He begins to focus on the steady thumping in his chest. The rhythm acts like a natural metronome and helps clear his spiraling mind. Tim exhales slowly; his mind is now blank, an empty abyss of silence.

The journal moves again, breaking the silence with the flapping of its pages. Without saying anything, Tim grabs the journal and starts ripping page after page. He doesn't look at the journal; he just rips pages out. The journal shakes and thrashes almost as if it's in pain. Tim ignores the journal's attempts to escape; his mind only lets him feel the pages ripping. Pages fly, some whole, some not. The sound of paper crumpling and ripping begins to resemble screams.

Eventually, Tim reaches the last page. The journal is barely moving now. It's weak. Tim can feel the journal dying. He takes the last page and gets a good grasp of it. He looks down at it and freezes. Despite wanting to end the journal here and now, Tim reads the final entry written in a dark burnt-red crayon. The handwriting is completely different from the rest. It's frantic and wild.

June 27, 2023 Log #125

After so many years, he's back. I didn't have to go looking for him. Had I known that starving his parents to death would bring him back, I would have done it years ago. He looks so handsome in uniform. He left a boy and returned a man. Seeing him like this gets me more excited than when he was sixteen. I better leave his room before he enters the house.

As I write this entry, my beloved Timmy is entering his childhood home. I have left his room and I will wait for him to come to me. In the meantime, I'll wait patiently in the basement.

Oh, the universe is rewarding my patience. Bless this wonderful day! He's back. Yes, my beautiful Timmy. My Timmy is back! Timmy is back! Timmy is back! TIMMY IS BACK! TIMMY IS BACK! TIMMY IS BACK! TIMMY IS BACK! TIMMY IS BACK! TIMMY IS BACK! HE'S BACK AND I'LL MAKE HIM MINE!

Tim finishes reading the entry and tosses the dying journal across the room. He turns to the small desk in his room and gets his backpack. He fumbles inside it until his fingers finally feel the cold steel he's looking for. He pulls out his handgun and darts to the basement.

With the muzzle front and center, Tim carefully makes his way down the stairs. Every step is methodically placed. His eyes cover every corner and possible hiding spot, from the vents to the inky shadows of the corners. He quickly turns right and passes the kitchen, then the home office. Tim presses himself against the wall before turning left to the final hallway leading to the basement.

He slowly steps up to the basement door and gently opens it. Not wanting to draw unwanted attention, Tim decides to not turn on the lights. With huge amounts of caution, he takes the first step down. His bare foot feels the wooden step, then the next, and so on. The darkness grows thicker with every step taken. Tim stops three-quarters of the way down so his eyes can adjust to the lack of light.

The process takes an excruciatingly long time. Given Tim's circumstances, half an hour of waiting feels like an eternity. Eventually, Tim feels comfortable enough to continue his descent, taking three more steps down. He can see the last five steps now. Carefully he counts in his head with every step, *One, two, thr—*

SCREECH!

The third step creaks like a rusty door hinge. Tim shifts his weight back to his other foot as quickly as possible, but the sound has already compromised his location. A heavy yet quick scurrying akin to a centipede reaches Tim's ears. The next thing Tim feels is a sharp pain behind both heels before tumbling down the rest of the stairs. The fall leaves Tim dazed and spread out face down on the ground.

"Hello, my Timmy. I've missed you," says a sultry, airy female voice. The centipede-like scurrying grows closer to Tim.

He reaches for his gun and turns around and as soon as he knows he's facing her, Tim pulls the trigger.

CLICK!

"Did you really believe that I would leave a loaded gun in your possession? No, my Timmy, it's far too dangerous," she says, still hidden in the dark.

Tim crawls backward, but a powerful hand pulls him by the leg. Pain runs up Tim's legs. He tries kicking, but his feet don't move correctly. They flop around like malfunctioning puppet legs.

Two hands grab his wrists while two more grab his legs. A heavy breath lands on his face as two more hands grope his chest. Her gentle touch drips with a mix of measured aggression and excitement. Slowly, two of her hands wander down to his hips. An uninvited kiss strikes Tim's neck, followed by an unnaturally long tongue sliding across his chest.

Tim tries to break free, but his strength cannot match hers. "No! Let me go!"

"Shhh! Don't resist, my beloved," she whispers as one of her hands covers his mouth shut. One of the hands on his hips slides down to his boxers. "We're going to have so much fun together. We'll make great parents, my love."

A Father's Pain

A FATHER'S PAIN

by Jose Francisco Trevino Chavez

"You lost, Richard. You owe me thirteen coins," Angus, the town drunk, slurs every word and smiles at Richard before downing the rest of his pint.

Richard, a gruff man who looks older than his actual years, tosses his friend the coins. "Debt paid. Hell of a hand, mate. Perhaps I'll get you next time. See ya around."

He stands up and heads toward the tavern's exit, struggling through the growing mass of buffoons attempting to drown either their demons in cheap liquor or their livers—something he knows he'll never accomplish despite his best efforts.

A few steps from the door, a rat skitters past, its ink-black fur shining a deep blue. A roaring bonfire erupts in Richard's chest, sobering him instantly. He grabs the knife strapped to his ankle. A split second later, the blinding rage is quenched as the plump rat writhes and squeals in agony. His knife pins it to the wood floor.

"Die, vermin!" Richard puffs out his chest like a raging bull. The tavern falls silent as everyone stares at him—all but one young man who continues eating his meat pie as if he hasn't heard a thing. Only the rat's dying squeals can be heard. Someone taps Richard's shoulder to get his attention but he doesn't budge. His eyes are glued to the rat as he takes in every second of bloody suffering. Finally, it stops clawing at the air, its head drops, and it dies.

Only then does Richard turn around.

Quentin, the new barkeep, stares at him. His young soft green eyes meet Richard's dark brown and dim eyes. "Oi, you all right? It's just a rat. You're scaring everyone."

"It ain't just a rat, boy. It's a precaution on my part." Richard moves closer to Quentin. "You weren't there." His eyes probe the barkeep. "What are ya? Nineteen?"

"Twenty as of yesterday. You're right, I wasn't there, but I know what happened. Everyone does. A lot of people's lives were destroyed that day. It's all right, you're safe." His tone is friendly, and there's a mellow look in his eyes.

Richard scoffs and wipes his thick mustache with a callused finger. "Don't matter, just get rid of it. I don't want to see another one of 'em. Ever. That clear?"

Quentin nods politely. "Yessir. Never again."

Richard steps on the rat and pulls out his knife. Then he wipes it on his leg and leaves.

Despite being drunk, he walks resolutely to the apothecary on the other side of town. The sky darkens from a lilac hue to a deep indigo. He arrives just as a tall woman is locking the door, her large brown hood making her look much larger than any woman could be.

Richard stands behind her. "I didn't know bears could use keys."

"What do you want, Richard?" She turns to face him, voice raspy. "You know my apothecary is closed at this hour."

His mouth opens briefly before closing again. He reaches for his belt and hands her a cloth pouch. "This month's coin. You see her soon, don't ya?"

She takes the money. "Like every month. Is that all?" Her gaze is cold.

"No. Tell her I miss her. Tell her I love—"

"Stop it, Richard. Please. She doesn't want to feel any more pain."

He sighs. "Mona, you know me. I would never hurt Emily. I know I failed her."

"You know that's not the reason my sister left you. Look at yourself—drunk every night. She lost her son. She won't watch her husband drink himself to an early grave. Maybe if you clean yourself up. Good night, Richard."

She walks away, leaving Richard with a bad taste in his mouth.

A week later, Richard is the first customer in the tavern.

Quentin looks up at him as he walks in.

"Harry spoke to me yesterday about the rat thing," Richard says. "I want to apologize. I shouldn't have spoken to you like that. Just keep the place clean. Please, I beg of you."

He's not a rude man. Most of the time, he sits in the tavern alone or plays cards with Angus. But today he feels almost…desperate. He brings a hand to his face and realizes he forgot to shave.

Quentin holds up the rag he was wiping the counters with. "No need for apologies, we're square. You feeling all right, Richard? You look glum."

Richard forces a grin on his stubbly face and nods, avoiding eye contact. "Peachy. Like everyone else here, it's the rats."

Quentin sets down his rag. "Why don't you tell me what happened? I've heard the story but not from someone who lived through it. One thing is to hear about it from a friend of a friend, but to hear it from the source… That leaves no room for gossip. We have time before the crowd arrives. Pints are on me."

Richard stops as he grabs the door, his large hand lets go of the handle. He turns back to Quentin and says, "Hard pass. Harry's ale ain't worth the pain."

Quentin smiles. "Is a glass of our best scotch worth it?"

Richard hesitates, his tongue remembering the familiar smoke foundation with layers of apple and orange peel. A tear escapes from his left eye. He returns to the bar. "Make it a bottle and I'll talk. But only because you ain't from here."

"Deal." Quentin reaches for the bottle and pours Richard a glass.

Richard downs it in one gulp and taps on it, waiting for Quentin to refill it. He does.

"I had a son. William was his name." He downs another glass. "Good Lord, it feels like that was a different lifetime. He'd have turned twenty-two next week. Around his birthday, I—I get a little on edge. He was seven when I lost him."

As Quentin pours another glass, he says, "Sorry to hear. What was he like?"

Richard smiles for a brief second. He shakes his head and takes the glass. "He was healthy as can be. Smart, like his mother. Brave little guy. Used to say he wanted to be a lumberjack like me when he grew up. I started taking him with me to work. My smallest ax weighed more than him. I planned on making him a hatchet. Never finished it." Richard wipes a tear off his face before it rolls down his cheek.

"Did it happen that year?" Quentin pours another round.

Richard nods, holding back a pout. "They came out of nowhere, those disgusting rats. They were everywhere. In the crops, the inn, on the streets, in the brothel, even in the wells. We did everything we could to get rid of 'em. Nothin' worked. I was chosen by the town to speak with the duke. He lived up in the mountains. Being a lumberjack, I'm used to the mountains and its forests. I explained the situation but he didn't care. Why would he? He had no rats. Not yet, anyway. I returned without a solution. We all gathered to form a plan. Those of us with weapons, we just started killing. I can still hear them, their disgusting little *pitter-patter* as they ran through town like a black wave."

Richard's bulky hand tightens around his glass. His eyes wander into the abyss of the past hiding in his scotch.

Quentin clears his throat and asks, "Richard, you feeling all right? I lost you for a second."

Looking up, Richard replies, "Huh? Oh aye, aye. I'm sorry. Guess the scotch is kicking in. We poisoned 'em, stabbed 'em, crushed 'em, but they just kept coming. Weeks passed, crops died, people got sick—some died. Eventually the furry demons reached the duke's estate. I tried to warn him, but by that point it was too late."

"Is it true his wife died because of the rats?" Quentin asks.

"No, she went to stay with her family. The rats ate his hunting dogs. Only left bones and collars." Richard slams the bar with one hand. "Only *then* did he decide to act."

Quentin flinches.

"Sorry, boy, just hate nobility. The town's problems ain't theirs until they're affected. All they care about is that we pay our taxes. To them...we ain't people. It ain't right. Anyway, he had his advisers inform the king. They took a while. We got good at killing those rats."

With a heavy sigh, Richard finishes his glass. His head droops and a strong surge of emotions run through him. His back tightens to the point of nearly ripping his shirt. He grits his teeth; a screeching sound escapes through his chapped lips. Quentin reaches for his glass to refill it, but Richard stops him. He wraps his muscular arms around the bottle like a dragon hoarding treasure. Quentin doesn't dare stop him; he just watches.

"Two months later, *he* arrived. Out of nowhere too, just like the rats. Our supposed savior. He was tall and thin, with a delicate grace like a dancer. He charmed his way into town."

"So, he was handsome," Quentin says.

"No, but most of the town fell in love with him anyway. Guess it was desperation. Can't blame 'em. I didn't mind him, but some men did. Insecure fools. He was dressed in black, so deep it looked like velvet, but something about it was different. Too dark for fabric. It looked more like a bottomless pit. He stood on the crier's spot and said, 'I've come to help. No need for payment, your duke will take care of that. He gave his word.'"

"And the flute?"

Richard nods. "Golden, he had nothing else. I don't know nothing about music but when he started playing...I know music can't do that. His music was—no, *is*—invasive. It forces you to listen."

"That loud?" Quentin asks.

Richard shakes his head. "Not loud at all. More like it nests in your head. The second the rats heard it, they froze. He cleared up the wells, then the crops. Took him two days. Seeing the way he controlled them...it chills the blood. That first night everyone slept like well-fed babes. But the second night was a different story. My son William came to me and my wife Emily that night saying he was having bad dreams. We held him until he fell asleep."

Richard runs his hand through his mostly white hair, his brows tense, buckling under all his burdens. He throws back his head and gulps half the bottle of scotch, then sets the bottle down with a heavy thud.

"I too started having bad dreams. The entire town did. I remember one where I was drowning in rats while my family called out to me. I could never get to them. I fought the rats in the dreams but I just couldn't reach my family. I'd hear that tune just before I woke up. I started to dislike that man. Felt like I shouldn't trust him. He wasn't normal."

Quentin's brow furrows. "What do you mean?"

"He played that damn flute day and night but no one ever saw him sleep. Didn't drink, didn't eat. Never looked at the brothel even though the owner gave him full access free of charge." Richard leans forward. "I saw him playing with a few of the rats. It looked to me like he was training them. He cleared up half the town and then went back to the duke."

"For payment?" Quentin asks.

Richard shrugs. "I'm not sure what happened there but it wasn't good. Something about the piper changed after that. His eyes—they were...odd."

Voices sound at the entrance to the tavern, Richard takes his last large swig of scotch and says, "Crowd's coming, we'll continue tomorrow with another bottle." He hands Quentin the empty bottle and leaves before Quentin can stop him, but not before he runs into Angus.

"Up for a game?" Angus holds up a deck of cards.

"Not today," Richard says and stumbles out the door.

At his workshop, he sits on a wooden chair he made years ago and lights himself a cigar. It's later than he realized. A half-moon shines through the window. *What if I had fought harder? What if I hadn't missed? What would William look like now? Would Emily still be here?* He loses himself in the labyrinth of 'what if's' his mind constructs every night and wipes his eyes after feeling the spider-like crawling of a tear running down his face.

Enough of this. He shakes his head, trying to loosen the ghostly shackles of the past. *Go to bed. You're drunk again. What would Emily say if she saw you like this?* He trudges upstairs. His bed looks cold, desolate. When he thinks of Emily—her copper curls, hazel eyes cradled under light freckles and a slightly tilted smile. Richard feels—a strong warmth fills his chest. He crumples onto the bed and curls up, howling in pain.

―ele―

The next morning, Richard gets out of bed and dresses for his usual workday. He stumbles a little down the stairs thanks to the hangover from all that scotch and wonders if he'll keep down his breakfast. His heavy frame slumps against the kitchen table. He takes a few seconds to regain his posture and continues walking to his first meal. He bends down and grabs the latch of the cellar door and pulls it open. The groaning hinge stabs at Richard's overly sensitive ears like rusty nails. It's dark. *Keep forgetting your lamp down there, Richard. Go on, it ain't like you're a fool or nothin'.*

In the cellar, he feels around, placing his hands on the wall and paying close attention to his fingered vision. Knives, hooks, aprons. *Where are you?* Finally, he locates the bottle-like container and a small metal rectangle. He finds the spark wheel and with one try lights his old brass lighter. The warm vermilion glow illuminates his surroundings. He takes the lighter and lights his oil lamp.

With the darkness finally tamed, Richard moves with confidence. A gentle clanking of chains reaches his ear. He moves his lamp to the sound. "Who's there?"

No response. He edges his way to the back wall where a smoke-dried pork leg hangs. When he brings the lamp up to the swinging pork leg, his breath catches in his chest. It's riddled with tiny bite marks, small chunks missing from top to bottom. When he lowers the lamp to illuminate the ground, something scurries away as if the light could harm it.

Richard's hangover disappears in an instant. That familiar worm tail makes every muscle tense in his body. He pushes an empty barrel out of the way and rushes to where the thing ran, lamp swinging every which way. Behind him, fabric rustles. He grabs the first thing available, a piece of drying firewood, and chucks it at the origin of the noise. The wood crashes to the ground as he makes his way over.

Beneath the fabric: nothing. He exhales sharply through his nose. As he continues searching, he catches something from the corner of his eye. Richard turns and sees it in one of the corners. In his direct line of sight it's dim, almost too dim to make out. He shifts his gaze ever so slightly off and tries to make it out.

Two green lights glow like fireflies. *What is that?* The lights are a bit lower than his eye level. Richard walks to them. Halfway there, it dawns on him: *they're eyes.* The hair on his arms stand straight up, while his heart races. *It's him!* He lunges forward. The light from his lamp reaches the corner before him, but when he gets there, it's empty.

His head throbs. He looks for something, anything, he might use as a weapon.

"Show yourself, bastard!"

But the light proves he's the only one there. He grunts and punches the stone wall. A wave of pain runs through his hand and up his arm. Halfway back to the stairs he sees the eyes again. He shines the light on the corner: nothing. *It's just stress.*

He leans on the wall behind him waiting for his heart to calm down.

I still see them. Every time he thinks they're there, he points the lamp directly at them and they vanish. He does this three more times, and each time they vanish. Richard smirks and thinks, *See? Just stress. Just like all the other times.* He breathes deeply and just then underneath the pair of firefly-green eyes, the taunting serene smile that haunts Richard to this day shows itself. Its unnaturally white teeth arch into a moon of a smile.

His blood runs cold. He wants to move but his feet don't respond. Out of the shadows, the golden tip of a flute peeks out.

"Today," a ghostly voice says, then a single note plays. A horde of rats run at Richard. His feet finally unglue themselves off the floor and despite him weighing over two hundred pounds, he nearly flies upstairs. He slams the door shut and sits on it as he latches the lock. The pests scratch at the door, their demonic squeals penetrating right through the wood.

Richard covers his ears and for the first time in fifteen years, he closes his eyes and prays. "Please Lord, I can't do this. Not again." As the scratching grows louder, he starts sweating. He remains seated, hoping his two hundred and forty pounds of mostly muscle will be enough to keep the creatures at bay. Tears start pouring down his eyes, and his jaw clamps down at full force. A sharp pain shoots through one of his teeth, yet he doesn't stop.

Richard has his eyes glued on the cellar door. He can *feel* them scratching, aching to burst through. His eyes bounce from one corner to the other. He spots a few whiskers slip between the door and the floor. He shuts his eyes and starts hitting his head over and over as he screams. His large hand slams against his skull, each time sending a numbing sharp-toothed shockwave across it. Several strikes in, dizziness replaces his blind terror.

Suddenly, Angus is there, yanking Richard back by his shirt. "Stop! Stop it! What are you doin'?"

Richard is disoriented. It takes him a second to remember, and the memory sends him right back down the spiral. "He's back! Run, Angus, warn the town!" He points at the cellar door.

Angus scratches his head. "Who's back? It's just us two, mate."

Richard grabs him by the collar. "The rats! He brought them back. He's not finished. Listen!"

Both fall silent.

Angus says, "I don't hear nothin'."

"Listen, dammit!"

But Angus is right. All Richard can hear is the chirping of the morning birds. "I heard them. I felt them. I saw them. And him—him too!"

Angus helps Richard to his feet. "Oi mate. You've been alone for years. I think it's getting to you." He puts an arm around Richard's shoulders. "Come with me. Let's talk."

Richard shrugs him off. "Don't give me that. I know what I saw. I'll show you." He opens the cellar door and leads Angus down slowly. Each step overflows with caution. His large frame is hunched over with his arms shielding his torso. *How can Angus be so relaxed?*

When Richard sees a growing orange glow, he hurries down. His oil lamp is shattered on the ground, the oil spreading flames a couple of feet wide where he dropped it moments ago. Richard turns to see how to put it out. He sees the large tarp crumpled up in the corner. In a second, Richard grabs the tarp and covers the small fire. Two harsh stomps and the fire's out. Angus reaches the bottom step just as Richard has doused the fire.

"What is it? I don't see anything. How can you even see down here?"

Richard reaches for his lighter and ignites it. "I saw them here."

"There's only us," Angus says.

"No, he—he was here. I swear it." Richard says while waving his hands.

"Who?" Angus asks.

"That monster, the flute player. The piper. He's back. I know it."

Angus stares at him. "You're seeing things again?"

"Not this time. I felt the rats through the door. I know I did."

"You've done this before." Angus reaches for Richard's arm. "Take it easy. Let's go upstairs." He leads Richard up to the kitchen. "Sit down and tell me what you saw."

"I—I saw his eyes. He hid in the shadows." Richard looks at the chair Angus pulls out for him but he can't sit. "All this time, he's been hiding right beneath my nose." He glances from one dark corner of the kitchen to the cellar door and back again.

Angus rises. "Let's go talk some other place. Come on, Harry will let us in."

Despite the hour, the tavern is open. Harry stands inside sweeping the floor. He smiles, his bald head shining in the lamplight. "Bit early, fellas. Even for you, Angus. Then again, business is business. What can I get you?"

Angus shakes his head. "We're not here to drink. We need to talk."

Harry sets down his broom. "What's wrong?"

Richard looks him in the eye. "The piper is back."

For a moment, there's silence. Then Harry walks to the door and locks it. "Richard, you need help. He's not back. It's been fifteen years. He'll never be back."

"Don't give me that." Richard hears his voice rise but he does nothing to control himself. "I saw him in my cellar. He spoke to me. You have to believe me."

Harry wipes his mouth but says nothing.

His silence burns Richard's insides. He turns to Angus. "You believe me, don't you?"

Angus sighs. "Mate, it's not that I don't believe you. I want to, I do. Look mate, I won't leave you. I—"

FEAR

Harry holds up one hand. "Enough. Don't humor him, Angus. We can't keep doing this."

Angus comes up close to Harry with his chest thrust forward. "Oi! Don't talk to him like that. You don't know how I found him. Look at him. He's the bravest man I know. He's trembling like a child. I ain't never seen him like this."

A knock on the door makes them all turn. Through the window, Quentin points at the doorknob. Harry goes to the door and says, "Give us an hour, son, we—"

"Come in, Quentin," says Richard. "The piper is back, but Harry won't believe me."

"What? We should warn everyone, Harry!"

Harry sighs and opens the door. "Get in. Quick." Before Quentin can say anything, Harry says quietly, "Nothing's going on."

"But Richard just—" Quentin lowers his voice too, but even from the corner table Richard can hear them.

"Aye, I know what he said. He does this every few years." Harry has the nerve to sound bored.

Quentin scratches his head. "Harry, look at him. I know I've only been here for a month but he's obviously frightened."

Angus nods at Quentin and tells him, "That's what I told Harry."

Quentin walks over to them and joins them at the table. "Hey Richard, are you all right?"

Richard shakes his head. "The town can't go through this again."

"And we won't." Harry turns to Quentin. "Look, son, don't mention this to anyone, eh? They'll just be angry at Richard. I know how to deal with this."

"Right, well... Perhaps it's my fault," Quentin says. "I was chatting with Richard last night. If I hadn't asked him, then he might not be like this now." He turns to Richard. "Apologies, sir."

Richard glares at him. "We never finished talking about it. You might as well know the whole story."

Quentin backs away. "Maybe that's not a good idea. Not after putting you through all this."

"Actually, maybe he should talk about it. Get it out, you know?" suggests Angus.

Harry crosses his arms but looks skeptical. "If it gets you back to normal, then start talking. But if it makes things worse, I swear..."

Everyone sits down and Richard picks up where he left off with Quentin. "When the piper came back, he was different. Started smiling at the children. Before, he never even looked at 'em. By the end of the week, he drove nearly all the rats out. It took him a little over a week to finish. Everyone, including myself, was so grateful. People bought him gifts, tried to give him money. He refused it all."

Harry brings him a glass of water, and he continues. "The day after the piper finished, he came to my home, asked me to escort him through the woods and up the mountain to see the duke. I'm the one who knows the fastest way to get there. I caught him staring at my boy. I ain't a scholar but I also know

I ain't no fool. His eyes...they held a warning. One I didn't understand until too late.

"We traveled through the mountains. Six hours to the duke's estate and he never said a word. I waited outside. He didn't take long. I'll never know the details of their meeting. What I do know is that it wasn't what the piper wanted. When he returned, everything about him was different. His posture, the way he walked, and his eyes—they held fire."

Richard takes a break. The memory is making him break out in a sweat.

"Take your time," Quentin says.

He nods. "I escorted him back to town. Asked how it went, but he never answered. When we returned, he said, 'Three days—or I'll take what's most valuable to you all.' He stood on the crier's spot with his flute ready to play. People tried talking to him, but he became a statue. On the third day, at around six, he said, 'The duke's actions are to blame.' He began playing. The tune was different, darker. I was eating supper with my family when it happened. William dropped his bread; his eyes became distant. It was Emily, my wife, who noticed it."

Angus puts an arm around him.

Richard hangs his head. "My boy stood up and left the table. I told him to finish his supper but he ignored me. I followed him out of the house and that's when I understood the piper's message. Every child able to walk was following *his* music. The piper was leaving town. I grabbed William to stop him. He bit and scratched until he escaped my grasp. He ran toward the music so fast I could barely keep up. They all ran. Every parent followed, but that was what *he* wanted.

"Before we knew it, he commanded the rats to attack. They ambushed us right outside of town. They came from the bridge across the river. If the first time was bad, this time was unimaginable. They bit and clawed us in a frenzy. It was like they were starved for that very day. Wave after wave came. It bought him time to escape. He went into the woods in the mountains with all our children. Arthur the huntsman and I were able to get past the rats."

Everyone leans closer to Richard to catch his every word.

"Arthur hurt his ankle along the way and told me to leave him. I caught up to the kids and that freak. He was sending them into a cave I'd never seen before. I managed to throw a dagger his way—but I missed him. I hurt one of the children, nearly killed her. I caught up to him and struck him with my ax across the face. He ran, but before disappearing into the cave, he yelled, 'I'll be back!' He ran inside and the cave disappeared in thin air! Neither he nor the children have been seen since. I've searched everywhere, but I don't know where they are. That cave isn't in the woods."

Quentin covers his mouth and there are tears in his eyes. Harry and Angus won't look up. A dense and somber second passes.

"What about the little lass?" asks Quentin.

Harry replies, "She's fine now. Richard carried her back here. I reckon you've seen her. She's the bakers' daughter, the red-maned shy lass. Diana."

Richard looks up and brings the conversation back on course. "I saw him today. The piper. He's back. We have to do something."

"Where?" Harry asks gently.

"In my cellar. He hid in the shadows and just like that...he disappeared. I saw rats too."

"Aye. There have been a few rats lately," Angus says.

"Call a town meeting," Richard says. "The townsfolk deserve to know." He goes behind the bar to refill his water glass and downs it in two gulps. "We can meet in the plaza. We'll pool all our weapons."

Harry grabs Richard's arm. "And then what? I know that day was the worst for most of the town but you aren't thinking clearly."

"Not thinking clearly?" Richard breaks free of Harry's grasp. "You didn't lose your boy. You didn't become a constant reminder of that day to your wife. Your marriage never crumbled. No, your son's curse became his blessing. I'm glad he never heard the piper, I truly am. Deafness saved him. You were spared from the town's hell."

Harry looks away. He can't deny it's true.

Grabbing Harry by the collar of his shirt, Richard explains, "This town has seen me spiral into despair. Aye, that day replays over and over again in my head. They judge me, turn their backs on me, even though I've never asked for anything. I just don't want anyone else to go through what I've been through."

"I didn't—" Quentin begins, but Richard stops him.

"Sure you and Harry pour my drinks but it's your job. You never ask how I'm doing." He nods at Angus. "But Angus here has never judged me. He's a true friend. My only friend."

Richard pulls Harry close. "I think about William every day. I haven't lost my mind. No sir, I'm sharp as a tack. I've been planning for this day. If you ain't gonna help, stay out of the way."

He lets go of Harry and leaves the tavern.

Back in his workshop, he grabs his ax, his lighter, some money, and a couple of daggers. As he exits, he's intercepted by Angus.

"I'm not sure if it's the right thing," Angus says, "but I wanna help."

Richard smiles. "Glad to hear it." He hands Angus a dagger. "Kill any rats you see. I'll meet you at the plaza in two hours."

"Aye, but why the change of time?"

"I was going to immediately warn the town. Harry's response reminded me of how the town sees me. There's something I need to do first."

He makes his way to the apothecary. As he arrives, a woman no older than twenty is leaving. Her fire-red curls hide her gentle face. The moment Richard lays eyes on her, he looks down to the ground. His chest tightens and he waits for her to pass. *At least you're safe. You were spared. Spared by my incompetence, but still. Focus!*

As he enters the apothecary, a cheery bell rings above him.

"Did you forget someth— Oh. What do you want, Richard?" Mona's eyes pierce through him.

"No need to be rude. I'm here to make a purchase."

"Really? You aren't here to ask about my sister... *again*? She already got this month's money. I'm not sending her any of your messages. The trip's too long. Once a month is my limit."

"I don't have the time for this again." Richard places a bag of coins on the counter. "Give me all of your strongest poison."

Mona stares at him. "For what?"

"Don't you worry, it ain't for me. Tavern's got rats."

"Fine. Wait here." Mona takes the bag with her into the back.

While he waits, Richard rests his ax against the wall and cleans the dirt from beneath his fingernails with the knife he keeps strapped to his ankle. He hears footsteps and a subtle hum that grows into a two-beat rhythm. He continues with his other hand, the blade gliding between his skin and nail. The mixture of sweat, dirt, and dead skin falls on the floor.

His head begins to throb, and the throbbing mimics the hum. It alternates from two beats to three then back to two. Two, two, three, two, two. His vision doubles as he recognizes the sequence.

He wheels around to the windows. "Show yourself, bastard!"

"Who are you talking to?" Mona asks as she returns from the back of the shop.

Richard lowers his knife. "I—I thought I heard something."

Mona frowns as he takes the box from her and leaves. *Keep it together. You know what to do.* He walks across town, stopping at specific spots to pour the poison. Around the apothecary, the mill, the well, the tavern. It takes nearly two hours, but when he's done, he makes his way to the plaza, dragging his ax across the cobblestones.

At the crier's spot, he rings the small bell. Slowly a crowd gathers. When it's large enough, Richard shouts, "Fifteen years ago, this town was robbed of its children by a monster. He has returned, just like he said he would. He—"

A rock hits him on the face. Richard lowers his head and covers it with his free hand. The sharp bite of the rock derails his train of thought.

"Stop forcing us to relive that day," a man shouts from the crowd. "You should be ashamed! You're nothing but a drunk."

Richard is tempted to launch himself into the crowd like a wild animal. He raises his head, ignoring the blood running down his now broken nose. He stares into the crowd and continues. "You've seen rats lately, I know so. The rats are back. *He* is back, and this time I ain't letting him win. I need your help. Who's with me?"

The crowd disperses almost immediately.

"You fling rocks at me yet refuse to heed the warnings! Shame on you all."

Angus arrives and stands beside Richard. Both hold their heads high despite the town turning their backs on them. "Don't you worry, Richard. You don't need 'em. What's next?"

Richard takes a second to wipe the blood off his face. "We go to the dam. Come on."

The dam is a long walk north of town. Richard leads Angus over to a boulder behind the bushes. Before them is a large wooden box with a long fuse.

Angus turns to Richard. "Is that what I think it is?"

Richard hesitates for a second. "Aye."

"You can't blow the dam." Angus pulls Richard back. "The water will destroy the bridge and drown all the crops."

Richard feels eerily calm. "I know." He looks Angus dead in the eye. "Trust me."

"Trust you? How? By the time we fix that dam, the crops will be long dead. Winter is nigh!" Angus grabs Richard by the shirt and pulls him away from the explosives.

But Richard breaks free. "I'm telling you, the end justifies the means."

Angus begins pacing. "The town's right, you've gone mad. I can't help you destroy our home." Without any warning, he pushes Richard down, grabs the box of explosives, and runs.

Richard shouts, "You won't stop me!"

"Watch me."

Richard sees him take off. With every step Angus takes, Richard feels a tightening of chains in him. Before he knows it, Richard is running after Angus. A well-placed tackle takes Angus down.

"What's wrong with you, Richard?"

"You can't stop me. No one *can*," Richard tells Angus before kicking him in the face. Angus loses consciousness. Richard drags Angus to a safe spot and returns to the dam with the box of explosives. He opens it, and checks the contents. A few sticks of dynamite and a pouch filled with powder. He lights the fuses of the dynamite, pockets a pouch filled with powder and goes to wait behind a large tree.

BOOM! The shockwave rattles the ground so violently it knocks him down. It takes him a few minutes to recover. Once he does, he walks back to town. People run past him, heading north, too preoccupied with the explosion to pay any attention to him. The whole town must have heard it.

Richard takes the long way back to town knowing the bridge will soon be destroyed. When he arrives, he walks around the perimeter pouring out the dark powder, then returns home. From his workshop window, he watches the townsfolk go about their business. A large group departs presumably to repair the dam.

Fools! He shakes his head and grips his ax tightly. Sundown paints the sky a rosy peach. Richard wraps his hands in bandages like a boxer. He lays out a few daggers and places his ax on the table. On the wall is the crude plan he drew of the town covered in small X's that mark key locations. He nods to himself thinking, *Just like you planned, Richard.*

He hides his weapons in his clothes and holds the silver cross hanging on his neck. Emily gave it to him on their wedding day. Pressing the cross against his forehead, he looks out at the darkening sky.

"Guide me, Lord. I just want justice. Please," though he wonders if the deity even exists.

Each second that passes creates a dreadful feeling inside him. The last glimpse of sunlight shows him his instincts were right. A rat squeezes itself out of the sewer and scurries across the street. *The sewers!* Richard glances at his map. *How could I forget the sewers?*

Another rat emerges, then another. Before he knows it, the street is overflowing with them, their ink-black fur pulsing like a rotting heart. He picks up his ax and pushes through the horde. *Tonight's the night. Do it for him. Do it for your son!* Richard takes a deep breath and lifts his ax to the sky. Letting out a primal roar, he swings it down into the rats. The ax head breaks through and into the street. A loud crack of stone mixes with the shrill and pain-coated squeal of the rats.

Richard continues swinging until he hears a scream and sees a light moving inside a house. "Run!" he yells. "Don't look back and run!"

As Richard makes his way to the church, the townsfolk become aware of the commotion.

With a good swing of his ax, he breaks down the church door. A wave of rats push Richard inside.

"Father Oz! Get up, now!" he yells. "The rats are back!"

But the rats are already squeezing under the door of Father Oz's chambers and his scream is cut short.

Richard runs up the stairs of the bell tower, trying not to think about Father Oz being eaten alive. His feet grow heavy with guilt, but the unmistakable sound of wood creaking behind him snaps him out of the fog. At the top of the tower he slams the door shut and slides his ax beneath the door's latch to lock it. The huge bell is his only companion. He grabs the bell rope and hangs from it. His weight sends the clapper swinging from one side to the other. The bell's thundering call reaches every corner of town. The sound is so powerful it tosses him to the ground.

Richard's world spins, his ears ring, and he struggles to regain his footing. A muffled squeal gets his attention. He looks around but can't pinpoint it. As the ringing dissipates, he figures out what the noise is. *The rats are at the door! Run! Now Richard!* He wobbles to his feet. As he yanks his ax from the door, it bursts open and a horde of rats surges in. He has no choice. He has to jump. He plummets immediately, his heft giving him nearly no air time. As he lands, his shoulder slams into a mix of cobblestones and ravenous rats. Something along the fall pops incorrectly, the razor sharp teeth of pain digging deep into Richard's shoulder. The vermin waste no time and begin biting. With one functional arm and his system full of adrenaline, Richard roars as he swings his ax like a wounded animal. The ax crashes again and again into the hungry mass of inky darkness. Orange sparks illuminate both the bleak night and the rage-fueled eyes of the small monsters.

"You want me? Fight me! You've taken everything from me!" Richard screams with every desperate swing. The rats move in unison, as if they're one creature. They come at him without mercy. As he fights and feels bites from every direction, the townsfolk escape their homes. But not everyone runs; some join the fight against the pests.

Arthur, the local huntsman, blasts through a bunch of them armed with his favorite hunting rifle. Their little bodies are no match for his hot lead. Otto, the baker and his wife, Nina, beat them with rolling pins. Between the thunderclaps of the rifle, Richard hears the wet crunch of rats beneath the rolling pins.

Their violence has rhythm, until the unmistakable sound of scraping metal interrupts the rat-destroying beat.

"Shit!" Arthur says.

Richard turns. Arthur's rifle is jammed. The rats immediately overwhelm him. He doesn't even have time to scream. The rats sever his jugular and drag him down into the sewers.

The only thing left behind is the rifle.

Richard tries to make his way to Otto and Nina but wading through the rats is like walking through molasses. Every step is a fight. But soon Richard and the couple are fighting the rats back-to-back. The more they kill, the more arrive.

The entire town is overrun. The townsfolk that didn't flee are either fighting in their homes or on the streets. The sound of glass breaking and wood cracking is now the town's ambient music, the vocals: screams. Richard can hear their anger, their desperation, their fear. Everyone is reliving the nightmare from fifteen years ago, only much more violent now.

As the rats retreat, Richard, Otto, and Nina lower their weapons.

"Can you hear that?" asks Richard. A rising pitch infiltrates his ears and nausea sets in.

Nina nods. "Yes. What is it? It—it hurts."

The pitch rises, sharp and piercing, without any sign of stopping. Richard takes deep breaths and searches for *him*.

"I—I don't feel good," Otto says before collapsing.

"Otto!" Nina cries out as she tries getting Otto to awaken.

The piper emerges from within the mound of rats and smiles at Richard. The long smile stretched out and over the man's scarred face sends shivers down Richard's back.

"Greetings, brave woodsman. I've come for more," the piper says, his bone-dry voice delayed by just a second, making his paper-thin lips move faster than his words. "Time has worn you down. You look ancient, fit for the role of a grandfather." He covers his mouth with his hand. "My mistake. No son."

Richard steps forward and looks directly into the glowing green eyes of the piper. "This time you ain't taking no children!"

The piper claps mockingly. "You didn't stop me then, and you won't stop me now." He pulls out his flute and plays a single note. The note shrieks, sending the rats into a demonic frenzy.

Nina is barely able to drag her husband Otto to safety. The rats charge, knocking Richard down.

As he tries to fend them off, the piper tells him, "Now if you'll excuse me, this street is far too noisy. I'll be over there, in the street without music."

He calmly strolls away, playing his pipe while Richard fights for his life. Rats crawl on him, biting and clawing. All he can see is the dark of night and the black rats. All he can hear is his ragged breathing and the rats squealing. Then...he hears it. The melody from that night. The night from fifteen years ago.

His insides twist. A fire ignites in him, and he swings harder and faster. He shuts his eyes and starts biting back. Warm fur catches between his teeth just as their skin bursts, sending mouthfuls of blood down his throat. With a burst of energy, Richard gets up and tosses the rats aside. He slams his ax head on the ground and yells, "You will die!"

The piper turns to him and runs. Richard chases after him but the piper's too fast and Richard quickly falls behind. He plays the melody from that night. The few people still in town fall prey to the piper's melody. Parents hold onto their children, but their strength is no match for the bewitching song. The children fight them off and break free.

When Richard sees this, he drops to his knees. "No. No! NO! NOOO!" Richard panics. He looks around and sees a limping man covered in mud. He's walking to Richard; the night and mud hide most details. A few feet from him, Richard sees it's Harry. "I can't stop him. He's too fast, too strong. And—"

"I'm sorry, Richard. We didn't believe you. But you...you can stop him."

Richard shakes his head. "No, my arm. It's useless." He pulls up his shirt, revealing one shoulder hanging much lower than it should.

"Broken?" Harry asks.

"No. Does it matter?"

Harry limps behind Richard and feels around Richard's shoulder. He takes Richard's arm and slowly swings it out. He takes the ax from Richard's good hand and places it in the other. "Don't let go."

"Wait, what are—"

CRACK! With a firm and quick pull, Harry resets Richard's shoulder back in its socket. Richard groans from the intense pain.

"Fixed," Harry says. "Now go, stop him. Please, Richard."

Richard stands up and shakes his head. He helps Harry sit down and then heads in the opposite direction.

"No, Richard. The other way!" Harry shouts but Richard keeps running. "Don't run away! You're no coward! Richard!"

Richard ignores Harry's shouts and speeds up. At the entrance to town he pulls out his brass lighter. The stroke of the flint wheel ignites a tiny orange beacon of hope. He kneels down and lights his way. His eyes follow the flame's light through the darkness until he finds what he's been looking for.

He steps back and places the flame directly on the ground. *FZZZZ!* The ground catches fire, sparks crackle and fizzle as the flames run. *Escape this.* Richard gets up and watches as the town is encircled by a huge ring of fire.

When Angus wakes up, his head throbs in a groggy protest. The night sky sparkles above him like scattered diamonds. It takes him a few seconds to remember how he got there. He stands up and runs to the dam but it is completely destroyed. A large crater shows him Richard's handywork, along with the wood and sandbags placed there by people trying to fix it.

"Goddamn, Richard!" Angus heads south to town when a sudden orange flash lights the sky. The town is surrounded by a towering ring of roaring flames. He is stopped by the river. The bridge to town has been washed away. He runs around to the other side, taking the long route home, but he can't get close to the town. Once there, he tries getting closer but the heat overwhelms him.

Angus looks around for something, anything to help him get through. It's then that he spots a steady stream of rats coming from the woods. Hiding behind a tree he watches as three rats run into the flames just before reaching the sewer. The rest of the rats stop and circle around, presumably to look for a new entrance.

He turns back and follows the rats' origin from afar. He walks into the woods and weaves through countless trees hiding sharp yellow eyes. It's then that he reminds himself of Richard's words: *"Remember that if you see eyes up above it's just an owl,* Richard told him once. *You won't have the chance to spot your predator."*

Angus pushes through his fear and after a while of traversing through the woods, he discovers the cave Richard talked about. There are too many rats to count. He waits for an opening, and once the rats are gone he slips inside. The light is faint but it's enough for him to see. It seems to be coming from a slender passage at the back. He follows the light to the back of the cave.

Angus pushes through the narrow path and into a large room with several cages hanging from the ceiling. At the center of the room is a glowing crystal ball, its light swirling in a pulsing rhythm.

There's a lever on the wall. He pulls on it and a loud grinding noise echoes throughout the room. The cages lower to the ground, allowing Angus to see the balled-up figures stuffed inside. The cages barely leave room for the inhabitants. He kneels down. A dirt-covered creature the size of a seven-year-old child stares directly at him. The child's dark beady eyes hold fear and innocence. He has scattered whiskers on a long, rodent-like snout, under a mismatched pair of ears. One is human; the other is large and round like a rat's.

Angus sees a large lock on the cage and asks the rat-child, "Where's the key?"

The rat-child points to the other end of the room past the crystal ball.

Angus follows the child's finger. The closer he gets to the crystal ball, the harder it is for him to focus. As he passes it, a metallic clanking comes from underneath the floor. A latch opens and an adult version of the rat-child comes out. When their eyes meet, both freeze for an icy second. The rat-man's eyes shift to the nearby table. Angus turns, following his gaze and sees a hammer. Both dash to it.

Angus gets there first, swiping the hammer to the ground. "Oi! I ain't no threat." Angus slowly raises his hands. "Relax, please. I don't want to fight."

"L-l-lie! Man b-ba-bad!" the rat-man shouts through a heavy stutter. He hits himself twice across the face and says, "He-he b-be angry if me no stop you!"

"He? The piper?"

"You know m-mu-music m-man?" asks the rat-man with a half-hopeful smile. "He save m-me when m-me small."

"You were a child, aye, but he took you. He's no savior. He's nothing but a thief."

"No! Lie, li-liar!" The rat-man charges at Angus, tackling him to the ground.

Richard can still hear the piper's maddening melody and can see the town's children following his every step. The piper leads his little zombies to the edge of town. He must not hear the hiss yet, but it gets louder and closer.

Finally, the piper stops walking and playing altogether. As he turns, a rush of vermillion heat crashes right through him. Scalding flames lick his slim physique, and he rolls across the cobblestones to put out the fire.

Richard towers over him. "Now, how are you leaving?"

The piper forces a scorched smile to his face. "You aren't man enough to stop me." He brushes the dirt off his charred clothes, lifts his flute to his lips and plays. The children turn in unison to Richard. The melody changes pitch, and immediately the children attack Richard. He steps back to dodge them but they are much faster than he is. They kick and punch. Richard pushes them aside with little effort; his large body is like a rock wall compared to them.

"Stop hiding behind children!" he yells while two kids bite him, one on the arm and the other on the leg.

The piper's melody now has a lower and darker pitch. The children start screaming at the top of their lungs. Their eyes grow red and they foam at the mouth. They attack Richard again, only this time they go for his neck, shins, eyes, and groin. They move like rabid goblins.

One of them bites Richard on the ear. He pulls the child off, tearing part of his ear with it.

"Ahh! Shite!" Richard screams from pain. *Do something. You can't stop him with the children fighting for him. Can't hurt them either, you're not like him.*

Richard steps back, covering his ear; the sharp pain radiates into his jaw. The same child prepares to charge at him again. He doesn't even look like a child anymore. He spits out the piece of ear he bit off and licks the blood running down his chin. The child runs at Richard, all innocence gone, corrupted and replaced by mindless bloodlust.

With a racing heart and his eyes tearing up, Richard drops the child with a sturdy knee to the stomach. *Forgive me, boy,* he thinks as the child loses consciousness. Richard fights each child. Each only needs a good blow to stay down. A kick, punch, or an ax hilt takes them out. No real damage, just enough to keep them down.

The piper claps. "Yes! Yes! Hit the children! What a hero! HAHAHA!"

His laughter cuts Richard deeper than a blade ever could. Richard charges at him, swinging his ax, aiming for the head.

The piper effortlessly dodges the ax head. Swing after swing, his graceful moves are like smoke swirling through the air. "Put some effort into it. You're getting close," he mocks Richard.

Richard takes another swing, he misses again. He keeps his eyes on the piper's feet, studying his dance. As he swings left, the piper moves right. He prepares another swing and just before releasing it, he fakes out and changes trajectory.

The piper catches the ax below the head. His ever-present smile disappears. "Clever man. Faster than you look."

A sharp pain strikes Richard across the jaw. The piper's flute is bent, dented. Richard's vision doubles as he falls to the ground.

"This is true speed," the piper says. "You didn't even see me swing. Pathetic."

The rat-man's sharp nails dig into Angus's arms.

"Stop it!" Angus cries, but the rat-man ignores him. Angus tries getting him off but simply can't move his arms or risk an injury to his neck.

From across the room, a voice yells out, "Stop defending him, Ed! The man's right and you know it!"

Ed, the rat-man, stops attacking and turns, shouting, "Shut it, William!"

Angus takes the opportunity and sucker-punches Ed, knocking him out. The key for the cages hangs from a hook on the wall. He grabs it and opens cage after cage. Nearly every person has rat-like features.

One of the freed rat-men says, "Thank you. I'm William. Let's get out of here. I don't want to be here when Ed wakes up. Do you know the way out?"

"Aye, the name is Angus. But we can't go back to town."

"No matter." William turns to the other captives. "Let's go!" William turns to Angus and says, "Wait, I need to stop him." He walks over to the crystal ball, raises it over his head, and shouts, "Rats we ain't! His control over us ends now!" He slams the ball to the ground and it shatters in a cloud of sparkles, sending a shockwave of warping light across the room.

The room falls silent. Everyone stares at him, eyes wide and hopeful. Just like the crystal ball, the silence shatters from an explosion of cheers. William follows Angus as he leads everyone out.

Richard clumsily crawls backwards as the piper walks toward him. He picks up Richard's ax and places his flute back in his bag. He drags the ax across the street. It scrapes and scratches the cobblestones; the grinding noise claws at Richard's ears until it reaches his skull.

"Fear not," says the piper, readying his first swing. "I won't make you suffer."

The ax flies down, missing Richard's groin by fractions of an inch.

"Now, now, quit moving and I'll end it soon. Promise." His words lag behind his thin smile. He places a hand over his heart. "What was your name again? That's right. It's Richard. In all my years of *pest control*, no one has given me such trouble. So many rats, children, and money, but never an injury. Then you came along." The piper points to his scarred face. "You did this. You disfigured me."

The piper swings for Richard's head but barely touches a few hairs.

"I still have him, you know." The ax rises. "I like him. Your little Will."

The words grip Richard's insides. He waits for the ax to drop. It flies by his face, nicking his cheek. He throws himself forward, he roars, his anger overflows through him. Tears drop to the street. From his roar spittle flies off. His hands grip the ax, the grip so tight his nerve endings beg him to stop as they send signal after signal of pain up to his brain.

"Yes! Yes, Richard! Let the beast out! Show me what you wanted to do fifteen years ago!" The piper's green eyes are bright with excitement.

Richard lets his rage take control. He slams his head into the piper's nose. There's a snap followed by a crimson spout on the piper's ivory skin. Richard continues slamming his head into the piper. Neither man lets go of the ax. They struggle like street dogs over scraps.

Richard can only see red smeared on white; he grows dizzy from the repeated head bashing. His air supply is cut off, his heart jumps to his throat. Confusion rears its ugly head, followed by the disappointing realization that he's caught a knee to the stomach. He slowly crumbles like the leftover ruins of a time-weathered castle. His heft betrays him as he crashes to the ground.

The piper stands over him with a blood-smeared grin under those unholy glowing eyes, and tosses the ax aside. "I want to see the light in your eyes go out. Go on, draw your knife."

Struggling to breathe, Richard asks, "How—how did—"

"I've been watching you. For years actually. I watched your marriage sink to the bottom of countless liquor bottles. Your wife must feel nothing but shame for you. I saw you in your cellar this morning. I saw you ruin the dam. I saw you prepare for me. Why do you think I came in through the sewers? I prepared too. Did you actually think you were able to survive my rats? No, no, no. I had them hurt you, wear you out. But I'm the one who's going to kill you. And don't worry, I'll take care of your boy. Now quit staring at me like a buffoon and draw your knife!"

Slowly, Richard gets up and draws his knife. *He's trying to get in your head. Don't let him.*

The piper pulls out his flute and lunges at Richard. He's too fast. He strikes like lightning. Pain buries its fangs in Richard's legs. Then his back, his shoulder, and ribs. Richard only gets in one swing before the flute catches him on the wrist. His knife clatters to the street. The piper picks it up and swings it at Richard, who trips backwards in an ill attempt to dodge it. On his back and facing death, Richard does the only thing possible. With an open hand he catches the blade. It pierces right through the skin, sliding between bones. The blade's nasty sting stops just before it reaches his face.

The piper puts all his weight on the knife. Richard pushes back; both men shake from the struggle. The piper's sweat falls onto Richard's face mixing with his own. Tears run down the side of his face as a thought confirms his worst fear. *You failed, Richard. You lost your son, your wife, your life, to him. You couldn't kill him.*

A shockwave of warping light crashes through town. The piper looks up and turns behind him, he turns back to Richard demanding, "What did you do? My rats!"

The onslaught of rats comes to a sudden halt.

Richard keeps pushing, blood trickles on his face. He can smell the iron of his blood.

"What did you do? Answer me!" the piper shouts again. "It doesn't matter. With or without magic, I'll kill you!"

Richard ignores the piper's shouting; his sole focus is survival. He keeps pushing, takes deep breaths and thinks about his life. The faces of his family pop into his head. Like a trapped animal, he snaps. *Now! Do it now Richard!* He knows his freedom has a price. With the twist of his body he shifts the knife sideways. The blade bites down harder as his hand twists with the blade still inside.

—ele—

Angus leads William and the others back to the outer edge of town. As they cross the woods Angus says, "The town is blocked by a fire. Walk toward the orange light."

"Can we put it out?" William asks.

"Perhaps, but we'll need to use the river. The problem is that all the buckets are in town. My friend, Richard, went insane. He—"

"My father's name was Richard. The last thing I remember from the day the piper took me is my father calling to me. The piper was badly injured by the time he returned."

Angus stops. He cups William's face in both hands and tries to see past the rat features. Then he embraces him. "Oh, child. It's you. It's really you!"

"What are you talking about?"

"You were taken from this very town. Your father is my friend. Come on."

Angus and William run to town with everyone else following.

A grunt turns into a groan, which morphs into a deep growl. Richard now mounts the piper and while holding the knife through his hand, he begins pummeling the piper's face with his other hand. The pristine pale skin soon turns red, then blue. The piper moans between strikes.

His knuckles grow numb. Something snaps—maybe his hand, but he doesn't care. The piper's moans are muffled by the gurgle of bloody saliva and loose teeth. Richard pulls the blade out; the pain goes unnoticed. Everything turns black for him.

Richard now sees both his hands wrapped around the piper's head. The flames around town are long gone. Some of the kids he fought stare at him with terror in their faces as he bashes the piper's head over and over on the ground to the point of breaking a few cobblestones. The deep black takes over once more.

When he returns, he finds himself using his silver cross pendant to strangle the piper. There is no resistance from the piper. He lies motionless, his eyes bloodshot, wide, and bulging. Richard knows the piper is long dead. He wants to stop; his body doesn't obey. Tears pour down Richard's face. Drooling over the piper's cadaver, he howls, "Give me back my son! You shite, give him back! Where is he?"

Richard sobs as he breaks down. His body is beaten and bleeding, yet it's his heartache that defeats him. His cries fall on both dead and deaf ears. The children he saved have left his side; the monster responsible for his pain has been slain. He buries his face in his hands and curls up like a child. Absolute silence surrounds him.

As the adrenaline fades from his body, Richard longs for death.

Suddenly, the silence is shattered. "Father? Father, it's me, William." A gentle hand takes Richard's and the same voice says, "Look, Father. I'm back, Angus freed me."

It takes Richard a moment to realize what the young rat-man has said. He barely looks up. His blank stare meets William's, the missing light shines in Richard again. His tired eyes see right through the rat-like twenty-two-year-old, finding his seven-year-old boy. He forms a weak smile that quickly shifts into a pout. Richard hugs his son, and the two break down.

"Your mother, she needs to see you," Richard says through his sobs. He stands, takes one step, and faints.

"William!" Richard cries out. He finds himself in his bed, his body aching from head to toe.

"I'm here, Father. I'm not leaving your side. Never again," William reassures.

Richard turns to his right and sees his son sitting beside him. "What happened? How did I get here?"

"Angus and I brought you here. You don't need to worry about the rest."

"No, wait. The piper—is he...?"

William takes Richard's bandaged hand. "Yes. He'll never take another child again."

"Thank you. I have wanted to hear that for fifteen years." Richard lies back down and stares at the ceiling. "Your mother should know about you. She doesn't live in town anymore. She moved back to where her parents live."

"I know, Angus told me. He also told me how you two became friends after I was taken."

Richard turns with difficulty. "Help me up."

William helps him sit, and Richard finds a clean shirt for himself. His silver cross pendant lies on the dresser, still stained with coppery brown blood. He sighs and says, "Let's go."

"You should rest. You're hurt," William says.

"This is more important. Besides, I have to apologize to everyone. Especially to Angus."

"About what? The dam? The bridge? The piper? Everyone will understand. And if they don't, then they are fools. I know Angus understands."

Richard smiles and hugs him. "I'm so glad you're back."

They go outside. The town is quiet, and there's hardly anyone around. Near the tavern Richard spots Angus speaking to Quentin.

Angus runs over as Richard says, "I'm sorry. I shouldn't have—"

"Shut up, you fool. You were right all along. I have nothing to forgive you for." Angus hugs him. "I'm so glad you got your boy back."

"Thank you. For everything, especially for helping my son."

"Don't worry about it. You're my best and only mate. Now go, I've talked to Harry about everything, and Quentin is helping us tell the rest of the town. There's people already out fixing the dam and the bridge. We're also trying to find everyone that was taken. We've found a few."

"I'll pay for everything," says Richard.

"Just go. Emily needs to know."

Richard nods and limps away with William to Mona's apothecary. The bell above the door rings and Mona looks up.

The ceramic mortar and pestle she's holding slip from her hand and shatter on the floor.

"Sorry I—I heard there was rat...er, people. I haven't seen one until now. Who's this, Richard?"

"Mona, he's back. My boy is back."

Mona stares at them, her brows dip and her nose scrunches forming wrinkles around her face. She walks over to them, avoiding the ceramic shards. "William?"

He nods, and she embraces him.

"What happened? Why do you look like—"

"We'll explain everything on the way," Richard says. "Will you take us to see Emily?"

"Of course."

Richard, William, and Mona travel to the nearest town South.

Along the way William explains everything. "After he took us, he kept us caged. He told us his hideout was impossible to find and that we should abandon all hope. He worshiped this orb. It's what made him powerful. His flute channeled its power. The closer we were to it, the faster we turned into rats. He kept me away from it so I could understand him when he watched you. He'd torture me with taunts, told me he'd kill you eventually. I'm just glad it's over."

"Me too, son. Me too."

The trip takes a total of three days by carriage. Along the trip, William's rat-like features fade.

When they arrive, Richard knocks on the door. He stands with William beside him and his hands begin to sweat.

"I'm scared," William says. "What if she doesn't recognize me? I can't picture her face anymore."

Richard kisses William on the forehead. "She'll know her son, anywhere. You will know her, too. And don't worry, I'm as nervous as you."

The door opens, and a petite woman with copper hair and hazel eyes stands before them. Her gentle smile disappears the second she sees them. Her hand covers her mouth, and she throws her arms around them, immediately breaking into tears.

"Thank you. Thank you. Thank you so much," she cries.

"I missed you, Mother. So much."

"My boy. My little William, you're a man." Emily cups William's face. She turns to Richard and kisses him.

For the first time in fifteen years, Richard no longer feels the stranglehold of failure. He's home, his family is whole, and the rats are gone—this time, for good.

SPECIAL THANKS

I want to thank everyone involved in the creation, distribution, and purchase of this book. Some of you worked with me on a technical level, some of you gave valuable moral support and some of you purchased it and or reviewed it. Whichever you provided, thank you. Thank you to the following:

To my mother who believed in me and saw the entire creative process.

To the other me. This should have happened in your lifetime too. I'm a man of my word, I told you we'd do it. I hope you're enjoying this as much as present time me is.

To my illustrator Falu, he designed the cover and the three illustrations. You can reach him over at Instagram at @faludisenios.

To Darling Axe Editing for editing most of the stories. You can reach them on X formerly Twitter at @DarlingAxe.

To Susan Russel for editing the story Timmy is Back and for formatting the book. You can reach her at SassyEdits.com

To Daniela Ricchezza for beta reading Timmy is Back.
To S. Kaeth for beta reading Dinner for Two.
To Kristi Wittmann for beta reading The Banquet.
To Emily, I hope we can see each other again. I love you.